A curious tingling was rippling through him now. In a calmer mood he'd have worked out a formula, something involving static electricity, and magnetic forces being drawn towards each other. But all Oliver knew was that he couldn't separate himself from the motorcycle or from Tony Edge, and that if he didn't break free he would die.

He started to cry, and the rider turned around. When the cruel dark eyes met Oliver's a stab of pain surged through him, and a lump stuck in his gullet. It was nothing to do with feeling sick, or the fact his throat was raw after all his useless pleading. The pain was in the terror, and the terror was in that face.

ANN CHEETHAM has written many books for young adults, including *Black Harvest*, which is available in a Dell Laurel-Leaf edition. She lives in England.

ALSO AVAILABLE IN LAUREL-LEAF BOOKS:

ANN CHEETHAM

# The Beggar's Curse

LAUREL-LEAF BOOKS bring together under a single imprint outstanding works of fiction and nonfiction particularly suitable for young adult readers, both in and out of the classroom. Charles F. Reasoner, Professor Emeritus of Children's Literature and Reading, New York University, is consultant to this series.

Published by
Dell Publishing Co., Inc.
1 Dag Hammarskjold Plaza
New York, New York 10017

This work was first published in Great Britain in Armada by Fontana Paperbacks.

Laurel-Leaf Library ® TM 766734, Dell Publishing Co., Inc.

ISBN: 0-440-91024-2

RL: 6.1

Printed in the United States of America

March 1987

10 9 8 7 6 5 4 3 2 1

WFH

For
Benjamin and Thomas

## The Ballad of Semmerwater

Deep asleep, deep asleep,
Deep asleep it lies,
The still lake of Semmerwater
Under the still skies.

And many a fathom, many a fathom,
Many a fathom below,
In a king's tower and a queen's bower
The fishes come and go.

Once there stood by Semmerwater
A mickle town and tall;
King's tower and queen's bower,
And the wakeman on the wall.

Came a beggar halt and sore:
"I faint for lack of bread."
King's tower and queen's bower
Cast him forth unfed.

He knocked at the door of the eller's cot,
The eller's cot in the dale.
The gave him of their oatcake,
They gave him of their ale.

He has cursed aloud that city proud,
He has cursed it in its pride;
He has cursed it into Semmerwater
Down the brant hillside;
He has cursed it into Semmerwater,
There to bide.

King's tower and queen's bower,
And a mickle town and tall;
By glimmer of scale and gleam of fin,
Folks have seen them all.
King's tower and queen's bower,
And weed and reed in the gloom;
And a lost city in Semmerwater,
Deep asleep till Doom.

William Watson

# Chapter One

Someone was hammering on the Blakemans' front door. Prill ran to open it, and tripped over a half-filled suitcase in the middle of the hall carpet. Her best friend Angela Stringer stood outside in the pouring rain. Her bubbly black curls had turned into limp ringlets, her anorak steamed, and there was a dewdrop on the end of her nose.

"I've come for the address," she announced, shaking herself all over the doormat, like a dog. "Can't write if I've no address. And you're off tomorrow, aren't you?"

*"Shut the front door!"* Prill's father bellowed from the top of the stairs. "It's blowing a gale up here. Come on, Colin, give me a hand with this will you." All that was visible of David Blakeman were two legs sticking out of the loft. Colin went up the stairs and grabbed one end of a battered trunk, and Prill steered Angela into the kitchen.

"Don't tell me about the riding lessons," she said, taking a pile of letters off the top of the fridge, "or I'll be jealous."

"Oh, I should think you'll be able to ride up there, it sounds very rural." Angela tried to sound encouraging. "Better than sticking to roads all the time—that's what I'll be doing. That's the trouble with a place like this, it's not the real country."

But Prill was determined to be miserable. The one compensation for having to spend the entire Easter holiday at home, being looked after by their grandmother, was the promise of a few riding lessons with her friend. Now it was all off, and Angela was going with someone else, because Prill had to go to Cheshire with her brother Colin, and their ten-year-old cousin, Oliver Wright.

It was all a big mistake, and Prill blamed her father. He was an art teacher who really wanted to earn his living painting portraits, and when he got a chance to spend his Easter holiday doing a retired judge, up in Scotland, it sounded too good to be true.

It was. There'd been a misunderstanding somewhere. The children liked the sound of the pine forest and the moors, there was even a river with salmon in it. But Judge Cameron's last letter had ended with a firm "P.S.": "By all means bring your small toddler, but we regret that we cannot accommodate the older children, or dogs, as we have dogs of our own."

Dad's second plan had been to ask Grandma Blakeman over to "live in" for three weeks. But that fell through too. At the last minute she phoned to say she couldn't come because the old friend she lived with had broken her hip and gone into hospital. Mr Blakeman was stuck. He couldn't persuade Grandma to leave her little house locked up, she was too worried about burglars and burst water pipes, and besides, there were two cats to feed, not to mention all the hospital visits. But he didn't want to give the portrait up, and he couldn't really afford to.

Then Oliver's parents came to the rescue. Grandma spoke to Aunt Phyllis and Aunt Phyllis spoke to Uncle Stanley. Why didn't Colin and Prill go to Cheshire for the holidays, with Oliver? He was going to stay with a relative called Molly Bover, who took paying guests and would be delighted to have all three of them. *And it would be so nice for Oliver*.

"Here's Uncle Stanley's letter," Prill said glumly. "And here's the address. Use the back of the envelope."

Angela nibbled her pencil and copied carefully, "Miss Priscilla Blakeman, c/o Mrs Bover, Elphins, Stang, near Ranswick, Cheshire." Colin had come into the kitchen and was reading the address over her shoulder.

10

"I wonder who 'Elphin' was?" he said.

"A saint." (Well, Angela's father *was* a vicar.)

"Really? It sounds more like a goblin to me. And *Stang*. Ugh, nothing very saintly about that. It's a horrible name."

"It isn't in the guidebooks," said Prill. "Dad looked. So it can't be very interesting. It looks quite pretty though, on these."

They spread Uncle Stanley's postcards out on the kitchen table. They were brown and faded, and had a faintly musty smell, like everything he sent them. Oliver lived in a shabby London terrace overlooking the Thames, in a small flat on top of a tall, thin house occupied by elderly people in bedsitters. Aunt Phyllis, his mother, was the housekeeper. She cooked their meals, made them take their pills, and ruled them all with a rod of iron, including Oliver.

"It's *very* pretty," Angela murmured. "It's got a duck pond with real ducks. And look at those nice old cottages . . . and those are stocks, aren't they? It's quite oldey worldey. What are you moaning for? I wish *I* was having the last week of term off, to go on holiday."

But Colin had turned one of the postcards over, to examine the back. Suddenly he gave a loud snort. "Stang Village," he read, "1938. These pictures are nearly fifty years old. Isn't that typical! Oliver's father's really stingy you know, he's probably been hanging on to these for years, 'just in case'. *Honestly*."

"Those ducks have probably died of pollution by now," Prill said gloomily. "There'll be a motorway running through the middle, I expect, and they'll have a petrol station, and a great big supermarket."

Angela laughed loudly. It was such a hearty cackle that even Prill smiled. Then she caught sight of the ironing board and pulled a face. "Oh heck, I promised Mum I'd have a go at that lot while she was out. She's got to pack up the minute she gets back, and just look at it."

"It's not too bad. You can just skim through it all, cut a few corners . . ."

"Angela," Prill shrieked, "we're leaving home at eight tomorrow morning, and the ironing in that basket goes back to the ice age."

Euston Station was like Oxford Street on Christmas Eve, and the train was even worse. Half the people in London seemed to be trying to get on, shoving and pushing and wandering grumpily up and down, looking for seats. And to cap it all, The Blakemans were late. The train was so full the guard agreed to let them put their dog in his van. She was a large Irish setter, lovable but mad, and crowds excited her. They were still trying to settle her down with all the parcels and packages when the train left the platform, and she was barking furiously at whoever walked past.

"Quiet girl, quiet," coaxed Colin. He felt sorry for the poor dog, squashed in between two bicycles with nothing to lie on and nothing to eat. "Molly Bover must be O.K.," he said to Prill. "She said she liked dogs, when she wrote to Dad. Gorgeous walks round the village she said, too. It could be all right."

Prill remembered the note, written on what looked like the back of a butcher's bill, in the most beautiful, flowing handwriting. "Yes, she did sound nice. Not a bit like a relation of Oliver's. Where is he by the way?"

"Up at the front. *In a reserved seat*. I bet Aunt Phyllis got him to Euston at about five o'clock this morning. We'd better go and find him, I suppose."

They followed their parents down the train. Prill soon lost sight of her mother, but there was no danger of losing Alison, her little sister. She hated the jolting carriages, the noise, and the big sweaty faces thrust up against her as people squeezed past. She howled solidly till Mrs Blakeman found a spare seat and sank down into it with a sigh of relief.

"I'll take the kids up to Oliver," Mr Blakeman said. "There might be a couple of spaces, you never know."

Alison bawled louder as Prill disappeared, and the sight of that crumpled little face made Prill want to bawl too. Her mother had told her to look on the bright side about this holiday. Alison had been a good baby but she was going downhill fast, and now she could walk nothing and nobody was safe. She broke things, pulled things apart, and yelled for hours when she couldn't get her own way. Grandma said she was getting herself ready for the "Terrible Twos".

But Prill loved Alison. She was twelve and her sister was one, but they were friends. She'd much rather put up with a bit of howling and mess than be dumped in some lonely village all on their own for three weeks. Colin was O.K., but *Oliver* . . .

There he was, installed in his corner seat, with his neatly labelled suitcase in the rack over his head, a small packet of sandwiches on his knees, and his nose deep in a book. "Hi, Oll," Colin said cheerfully.

"Oh, hello. You made it then. Good job I kept these." Across the aisle were two empty seats, one occupied by a yellow bobble hat, the other by an anorak.

"Thanks, Oliver," Mr Blakeman said. "That was clever of you."

"It wasn't my idea," the boy said coolly. "My mother did it. She knew you'd be late."

"Well, you saved our bacon anyway. I had visions of us all standing up for three and a half hours. Now I'm going back to your mother," Mr Blakeman told Colin and Prill. "I'll pop back, but you know we get off at Crewe, don't you?"

"Of course I do," Oliver said quite irritably. "That's where Molly's picking us up." And he pointedly turned the page of his book.

Mr Blakeman vanished. The brother and sister exchanged looks, then they both glanced across at Oliver. "He's not improved much, has he?" Prill whispered. "He looks as weedy as ever. And why does he always dress up for an antarctic expedition? It's not that cold."

They hadn't seen Oliver since last summer, but he was much the same; a bit taller perhaps, but still pale and droopy-looking, and thin to the point of boniness. The glasses were new. Behind them his pale bulgy eyes gobbled up the print. They were large eyes, a curious washed-blue colour, with the hardest, coldest stare they had ever seen in anybody. "What are you reading, Oliver?" Colin said.

There was no answer. He simply held the book up so they could see the title. *Cheese and Churches—Rural Traditions in Cheshire*.

"Any good?"

"I don't know yet. I've only just started. It's my father's."

Uncle Stanley was a schoolteacher like Mr Blakeman, but the kind that specialised in being boring. Oliver's school had long holidays, a whole month at Easter which his father usually filled with special "projects". It was his own fault that his son was such a swot.

*Cheese and Churches* was obviously much more interesting than talking to the Blakemans, and Oliver clearly planned to read for the whole journey. To a normal person Colin might have said something like "Don't speak, will you," or "I'm used to being ignored." But this was Oliver. He could be friendly when it suited him, even fun, now and again, but most of the time he was a loner.

It took a long time to get to Crewe. At every halt the train lost more and more time, and Dad's idea of a fond farewell before they all split up faded gradually into nothing. The connecting train to Scotland would not be kept back, and the guard reckoned it was "a fair old walk" to the next platform.

So goodbyes were said hurriedly in the corridor as the train slowed down, and it was just as well. Prill was in a black depression about the whole thing, she wanted to go to Scotland with her parents, and Oliver seemed worse than

14

ever. At least it had been their holiday, last summer, and he'd been a guest. But this Molly Bover was his father's cousin, Oliver had been to Stang once before, and the Wrights had farmed in Cheshire for years and years. He'd be bound to make the most of it, parading his knowledge. He was such a little know-all.

Prill shut her ears to the last goodbye and turned her back on the final glimpse of her parents, rushing after a man with a trolley. After all the fuss of getting off, Crewe Station seemed strangely quiet and she stood alone, feeling like a little lost boat washed up on a sunless beach.

Then a voice said, "Oliver, hello dear. I was late, as usual. But I'm here *now*. And this must be Prill? And you're Colin? I'm Molly Bover." An irate railway official was coming towards them with Jessie on the end of a lead. He thrust it irritably into Colin's hand. "Here, take it will you. I've had enough of this dog. It's been a perishing nuisance. Noisy devil."

Jessie was overjoyed to be free. She barked loudly and leaped up at the three children, wagging her tail and slobbering.

"Steady on," said Molly Bover, taking a step back. She was a large lady but Jessie was almost knocking her over. "Gorgeous dog, but who's is it? And where's that man gone? Surely someone's looking for it?"

"It's ours," said Colin.

"Oh, but—*yours* dear? This?"

"Well, yes; she wasn't allowed to go to Scotland, you see, and you said . . ."

Molly Bover's round moon face clouded slightly. She said nothing for a minute, but took refuge in the three young faces. She liked children. The two Blakemans looked alike, freckled and gingery with curly reddish hair and dark brown eyes. Prill was pretty, a good subject for a portrait. But Molly didn't paint these days, she had to concentrate on making her pots, to bring a bit of money in. Next to his cousins poor Oliver looked a real shrimp.

15

Colin was a head taller, broad-shouldered and powerful-looking. Oliver was pale-faced and spindly.

Molly thought he spent far too much time on his own, shut away in that damp little flat with his mother always pumping pills into him. A week or so in the country would do him a power of good . . . Her reverie was shattered by a shaggy wet face being thrust under her nose, and by more mad barking. "*Jessie*, of course, yes, I do remember now. Only there are the poodles . . . Oh well, let's sort that out when we get home. Come on."

They followed her out of the station towards an old blue estate car, Oliver carrying his tidy little case, Prill hanging on to the dog, Colin gloomily lugging a trolley with their old trunk on it. He had that sinking feeling. Molly Bover had obviously forgotten about Jessie and the dog wasn't used to other animals. She'd eat Poodle One for dinner and Poodle Two for tea. It wasn't a very promising start.

# Chapter Two

The minute the car door was opened all hell broke loose. Two toy poodles in the back hurled themselves against the battered dog guard in their efforts to get at Jessie. She barked back, leaped on the nearest seat, and pushed her long nose through the bars.

"Jessie!" Colin yelled, yanking her outside. He could see the guard collapsing and the whole thing ending in a bloody free-for-all.

"Get in, get in, will you," Molly said, vaguely alarmed. "I'll put the cases in the back. Can she sit with you, do you think? It might be easier."

Oliver settled himself by a window and the others clambered in after him. Jessie scrambled up on to the three pairs of knees and squirmed round trying to get herself comfortable. She liked being with people.

Oliver was almost suffocated. It had taken him all last summer to get used to this dog, and she'd obviously gone backwards in the last six months. The Blakemans just didn't discipline her. And he didn't like having the tail end either. He gave Jessie a sly shove and she moved over slightly, making herself into a miserable russet heap on Prill's lap.

Colin thought Molly Bover was a bit odd-looking. Dad had told them she was over seventy, but in spite of the thick white hair straggling out of its untidy bun, she had a young face. She wore a dusty black cape with a hood lined in bright red. The hem was falling down and pinned up with a few safety pins. The artistic effect was further ruined by some mud-spattered wellington boots.

Uncle Stanley had warned them to expect bad weather up here, he'd advised rubber shoes, hats, gloves, and hot-water bottles. Oliver, who always wore three times as many clothes as anyone else, was obviously well-prepared.

The two black poodles were called Potty and Dotty and they yapped solidly all the way home. Colin and Prill grinned when they heard the names. It was hard to picture this sensible, no-nonsense Molly Bover yelling "Potty! Dotty!" down the village street. It was a long drive from Crewe across the flat Cheshire plain. The road threaded its way across a patchwork of small fields and went through villages of rather dreary houses. Now and then they saw a thatched cottage painted white, criss-crossed with old black timbers.

"Magpie architecture," Oliver said importantly. "It's in my book. They built the houses like that to make them more stable. The ground's not always too firm, round here."

Prill scowled at Colin. *He was off*. Why, oh why, did Grandma's friend have to be in hospital *now*, just when the holidays started? She'd forgotten how irritating Oliver could be.

They kept seeing signs to Stang but there was no sign of a village. The car rattled down narrower and narrower lanes, then dived under a bridge. "There's a canal above our heads," Molly explained, slowing down so they could see properly. "It leaks a bit. When I was a child I used to stand here and imagine the whole thing collapsing. Anyway, we'd better get on. Not much further now."

"But where *is* Stang?" said Prill. They'd emerged from the dripping bridge on to a perfectly flat piece of road. "It's miles away, surely?"

"*Wrong*," Molly answered mysteriously. "We're nearly there. It's in a valley, you see. You can never see Stang till you're right on top of it. I expect your dad's told you the old rhyme, Oliver?

'The last man into Stang at night
Pulls down the lid and makes all hatches tight.'

18

He was always quoting that."

Prill felt cold. It would be warmer down in the village, nicely tucked away in its little hollow. She was quite relieved that Stang wasn't up on this plain where the wind could get at it, or near that gloomy canal. She stared through the window as Molly slowed down to let a tractor go by. Spring had hardly started here yet, though it was a very late Easter. The trees were only the faintest green. It was as if they were waiting for a warm spell, before hanging their flags out. For April the countryside was unusually quiet and still. Spring was well advanced at home, with trees in full blossom and birds busy everywhere. Round here, everything seemed to be still waiting.

Molly had switched her car engine off. A three-sided argument had developed between the tractor driver, a builder's lorry, and a loud-mouthed youth on a red motorbike. "Sorry, folks," she said cheerfully, opening her window. "A bit of local colour for you. That's Tony Edge, our local Romeo."

"A great big scrape," the boy was bawling at the lorry driver. "Have to be resprayed that will." Then they heard, "Come off it, mate, you did it on purpose. I know your sort."

"Oh, he is ridiculous," Molly muttered through her teeth. "As if the poor man *meant* to do it. Come *on*, Tony," she shouted. "Move, will you. I've not got all day." And she gave a sharp blast on the horn. At the sudden noise the young man jerked up his helmeted head and stared at the rusty old car ferociously. Colin was peering out of a side window, and their eyes met.

There was something rather awful about Tony Edge's face, though he was certainly handsome, tanned, with bold, even features, large eyes, and a good strong nose, and he'd recently grown a splendid moustache. No wonder all the village girls wanted to go out with him.

But it was his eyes.

Colin tried to outstare them, but he couldn't. Something in that face forced him to drop his gaze and he peered down into his own hands, feeling vaguely foolish, not really understanding what was going on. He was shivering slightly, and his flesh tingled as if he'd just had a small electric shock. That awful stare had made their cousin's cool, calculating look seem quite ordinary.

He glanced at Oliver but all he could see was a narrow back. His cousin got dreadful car sickness. Perhaps he was taking this opportunity to vomit out of the window. Poor Oll.

But Oliver was doing no such thing. He wasn't interested in a slanging match between a village lout and a man in a lorry. He'd seen something much more interesting, and he wanted to take a photo of it.

Oliver was often very secretive; he slid a small camera out of his pocket, pressed the "telephoto" button, and put it to his eye. His ignorant cousins would say it was only a sparrow, but Oliver thought that the small bird hopping in and out of the tangled hedge might be something much rarer. He breathed in, and clicked. It was the last film on the cartridge so he could get it developed quickly and sent off to his father. Just because they lived in London it didn't mean he wasn't interested in wildlife. He knew a lot more about birds than the Blakemans, anyway.

Molly rammed her foot on the accelerator and they bumped noisily down the hill into Stang. The valley was quite large. Church, green, and duck pond formed the village centre but the road went on going down for some while, then turned up sharply, petering out in an old footpath called Coffin Lane. "There was a tax on salt in the old days," Molly explained, "and they're supposed to have smuggled it out of Stang in coffins along this track. Hence the name. I bet there were a lot of funerals!" At its lowest point the track bordered the edge of a deep pool called Blake's Pit. This was the real heart of the village, she said, and several families still lived there, including the Edges, in houses above the water that clung for dear life to the steep valley sides.

"It's a grim old spot," she muttered, turning in at a gateway. "Walk down later and have a look. Can't say I'd fancy living there myself though. I like it up here, where the life is. Welcome to Elphins anyway, dears. Can you sort yourselves out? I'll just go and find Rose, and I'll bung the poodles in the shed for a bit, so you can bring your dog in."

"It's the best house in the village," Oliver said firmly. "My father said so."

"Elphins" was a rambling old place, black and white with a mouldy thatched roof in such bad repair it looked as if giant moths had eaten great holes in it. It was set well back from the road, in a tangled wilderness that must once have been a garden. Prill and Colin looked at it in dismay.

"It obviously needs money spending on it," Oliver said defensively, "but Molly's not got any. That's why she does bed and breakfast. Anyway, *I* like it." And he lifted his suitcase out of the car and went up the path. The other two weren't at all sure. Silently they manoeuvred their trunk out of the back and dumped it on the gravel. "You take that end," said Colin. "It's not too heavy." But as they struggled with it he suddenly felt eyes on his back, and, glancing over his shoulder, he saw the face of Tony Edge staring across the road. The same strange feeling began to creep over him again, making him shiver.

"Hang on," he lied to Prill. "I've not got hold of it properly. Let's put it down for a minute," and he turned right round and gave the face a good stare. But it wasn't Tony at all, this boy was younger, about thirteen, much squatter and more thickset, wearing an old donkey jacket and a dirty baseball cap. But the face was the same, and the same hard, dark eyes were boring into him, making his hands sweat. It was uncanny.

"Look, have you got it?" Prill snapped. "Because I'm cold. . . Well, *come on* then."

21

All the time they were at the car the boy lolled against his fence, watching the proceedings with intense interest. Then the church clock struck six and he stood upright, straightened his cap, and stared up the road. But someone was coming towards them; he suddenly put his hands back in his pockets and slouched against the fence, watching.

They saw the little figure creeping along, a small brown person enveloped in a dingy raincoat and carrying shopping. One hand held a plastic carrier with celery sticking out of the top, the other clutched the handles of an old-fashioned carpet bag.

"Hello, Rose," the boy called out. She stopped and looked up. Her hair was tucked out of sight inside a brown knitted pixie-hood that buttoned under her chin, and they saw a small oval face, smooth and freckled like an egg. It was hard to work out how old she was, she might have been twenty, thirty, or anything in between. "Want me to carry your bags then?" the boy hollered, and stepped forward.

"No . . . no . . ." Rose stammered. The sad little face didn't look anxious any more, it looked terrified. She started to run but just outside Elphins the road was still cobbled and the ancient stones were loose and dangerous. Rose tripped and fell flat on her face. She clung grimly on to the carpet bag but the carrier landed on the cobbles. "Me eggs," she whimpered. "All me eggs. Fresh today an' all."

As the sticky yellow mess oozed out on to the road she started to cry. The boy by the fence laughed loudly. "That's typical of you, Rose Salt," he sneered. "You can't even carry a bit of shopping home. Cheshire born and Cheshire bred, Strong in th'arm and weak in th'ead. That's you." And he set off, up the street. Rose, still spreadeagled on the stones, sobbed harder than ever.

The two children were so taken aback they just stood by the car, goggling, but Rose's wails had brought Molly out of the house. "It doesn't matter at all, dear," she said

22

gently, helping Rose to her feet. "It wasn't your fault. Come on in now, our visitors have arrived. And I saw you'd got tea ready, now that was clever of you, dear." Then she called up the street in a very different voice. "As for you, Sid Edge, you're Cheshire born too you know, just in case you'd forgotten. Thick as a brick, like all the Edge family," she whispered to the two children, steering the sniffling Rose up the garden path.

"Who *is* Rose Salt?" Colin asked Oliver, when they were getting ready for bed.

"I don't know. My father never mentioned her. I didn't know she lived with Molly."

"I think she's a bit weird." Colin was jumping up and down as he pulled his pyjamas on. "This place is freezing. Do you think Molly would mind if I filled my hot-water bottle?"

"Why should she?" Oliver was putting a pair of thick red socks on, to wear in bed. "She's not the touchy type, you know."

"No, she's nice. But what about *Rose*, Oll? She gives me the creeps. And why does she wear that funny hat all the time? Do you . . . do you think she's *bald*?"

The two boys collapsed into giggles, then Oliver pulled himself together sharply. His mother wouldn't approve of that kind of joke, she was rather religious. "I don't know. She's definitely a bit odd. Perhaps she's the village idiot," he said slowly.

"*Oliver*, what a thing to say."

"Well *you* said she was creepy," he said huffily, tucking a scarf round his neck and climbing into bed.

Prill couldn't get to sleep because of the cold. If this house didn't warm up soon she'd spend the whole holiday in the kitchen. It had an open fire, and she quite fancied sleeping down there tonight, with Jessie. Colin's stuff had been in the top half of the trunk. He'd unpacked, then dragged it along the creaking corridor to her room. There was something in the bottom that she hadn't wanted anyone to see, and she was clutching it now, an old French doll called Amy.

Amy was the most precious thing Prill had. Her grandmother had given it to her on her tenth birthday. It was an heirloom, brought back from World War One by Grandad Blakeman's father. Prill was too old for teddies and stuffed toys, and this doll usually sat on the shelf at home, above her bed. There was nothing cuddly about Amy, with her disapproving porcelain face, her frilled dress and her real leather shoes.

But she smelt of home, and Prill needed something to remind her of Mum, Dad and Alison. She'd only once been separated from them all before, and it was only for a day or so. She knew she wasn't going to enjoy this holiday very much, and she didn't like this cold, dark house either.

Much later, when someone crept into her room, Prill was still awake, though Stang church clock had already struck midnight. When she heard the door open she half closed her eyes and took deep, regular breaths, though her heart was thumping, and she peeped at the figure hovering near the bed.

It was Rose Salt, still in her pixie-hood, but now wearing a long yellow nightie. She stretched out a little brown hand and touched the doll's blue frills, then ran a finger over the painted face. A tiny sound escaped from her lips. "Ah . . . *Ah* . . . she was sighing, tenderly. But at that moment Prill turned over quite violently in the bed, closed her eyes properly, and clutched the little French doll much tighter.

# Chapter Three

Molly Bover was a great leaver of messages. Colin came down first next morning and found the kitchen table covered with little notes. *One*: She'd gone off at seven, with the poodles, and taken a carload of pots to a craft fair near Chester. *Two*: She would drop Oliver's film into "Kwik Flicks", a new rapid-developing place in Ranswick. *Three*: Breakfast was on the stove. *Four*: Her old friend Winnie Webster was expecting them for lunch at twelve-thirty sharp. Her bungalow was easy to find, they just had to follow their noses to Blake's Pit. "DON'T BE LATE!" she'd added in curly capitals, decorating the exclamation mark with a skull and crossbones.

There were no notes for Rose Salt. Perhaps Oliver was right, perhaps she was a bit weak in the head. She probably couldn't read. Colin looked all round, but there was no sign of her. The long brown mack had gone from its hook on the back of the door, and the carpet bag had vanished too.

He helped himself to porridge and buttered a pile of toast. If Rose had made the nutty brown bread she could certainly cook. Colin ate so much it was quite an effort to get up from the table. Then he remembered Jessie. Molly had put her in the shed in exchange for the poodles—quite a comedown, after queening it all night by the kitchen fire. She was overjoyed to see him and made a lot of noise. He clipped her lead on and they set off along the village street towards the church.. Prill thought his fascination for graveyards was morbid, but Colin quite fancied being an archaeologist, and if you wanted to work out the history of a place you should begin with its church, according to Dad.

Every cottage seemed to have two or three cats and Jessie barked systematically at every single one. As he walked past the village shop a man flung open an upstairs window and bellowed, "Keep that dog quiet, will you!" The shop front was very shabby, and all the blinds were down. "Edge Brothers, General Provision Merchant, High Class Butchers and Poulterers" was written across them in white. It looked anything but "high class". It was nearly nine o'clock but there were no signs of life at all, and it wasn't Sunday.

The man at the window was still in his pyjamas. His eyes followed Colin along the street and watched him turn up into the lane that led to the church. The boy's neck prickled. One quick, backward glance had revealed the Edge face again. It was as if some demon farmer had gone round Stang with a giant butter pat, stamping his mark. It was the same look, the same stare, the same eyes. Awful.

When he saw the church he did another double take. On top of a square, chubby tower there was an elegant steeple, but it was definitely crooked; in fact it was toppling to one side quite alarmingly, like the leaning tower of Pisa. The church was obviously under repair. There was a concrete mixer by the door, a litter of scaffolder's poles, and some piles of newly cut sandstone blocks, all marked with numbers. A man in overalls climbed down a ladder to talk to him.

"Looks dreadful, doesn't it?" he said with a grin. "Don't worry, son, it won't fall over."

"Are you underpinning?" Colin asked, rather pleased with himself for knowing the right word.

"Oh no, now that really would mean rebuilding, digging into the foundations, and all that lark. No, the spire's safe enough. They watch it, you know. Lots of buildings lean a bit, in Cheshire. It's the old salt workings."

"Yes, I know." Cleverclogs Oliver had told them that.

26

"We're just renewing some of the stonework on the tower. Some old woman died recently and left this place all her money. Good for trade, of course." He started to go back up the ladder. "You could come up and have a look tomorrow, *when the boss isn't around*," he added in a whisper, pointing a finger heavenwards to a pair of legs.

"I might . . . Thanks," Colin said. But as he watched the man crawling spider-like up the underside of the toppling spire he felt quite sick and closed his eyes. It was such a delicate steeple and it leaned so horribly. He could see the weight of the cheerful builder dragging the whole thing down . . .

For a while he wandered round the churchyard, looking at the graves. Everything was very overgrown; daffodils had speared up through the grass but they were still tightly closed, and the trees remained a sullen brown. How cold and damp it all was. He had no gloves, scarf, or hat. Just for once he quite envied Oliver all those winter woollies.

The graveyard was dominated by three names, Edge, Wright and Bover. Others had come and gone, but these families had obviously been around for centuries. There were dozens of Wrights, and about twenty Bovers, but the Edges outnumbered everyone else. It was as if they had a stranglehold on the village.

Colin noticed that several people in Stang had lived rather short lives. One stone marked the death of a James Weaver in 1803 "Whom Neptune Deprived of Life". He was only seventeen. There was an Isaac Bostock and his son Samuel who had both died "pitifully", in a drowning accident. Where? Could it have been Blake's Pit? But there was nothing to say. Most pathetic of all was the grave of the three Massey children, "tragically lost" on the night of April 21st 1853. How and why they were "lost" the crumbling headstone did not reveal.

The Edge clan, on the other hand, had obviously enjoyed rude health. They'd had large families and most of them had lived into ripe old age. This dank, cold village in the valley bottom obviously suited them perfectly.

At ten o'clock Oliver was walking towards Blake's Pit with a thermos flask under his arm. Molly had left it out for Rose to take to a sick old lady in the village. "Now I'll leave it ready on the kitchen table," she'd said last night. "Rose? Are you listening, dear? Don't forget it, will you? Miss Brierley likes her drop of soup. Now *don't forget it, Rose.*" But she had, and Oliver had found the red flask still on the table. He didn't mind taking it to Miss Brierley's cottage, he was quite used to old people, and they didn't bother him in the way they seemed to bother his cousin Prill. She'd pulled a face when Molly suggested they might drop in on this old lady, now and again.

Her tiny cottage was called Blake's End. It was easy to find because it was the very last house in the village. The only other place anywhere near it was an untidy farmhouse, with an ancient caravan in a field at the front. This was Pit Farm where Tony and Sid Edge lived with their parents and their sister Violet.

The caravan was apparently let to a family of cousins. It was moored at the edge of a great sea of rusting machinery, old radiators, car tyres, and lumps of old iron. Oliver walked past slowly, to get a good look. In a place like Stang there might be some old farming tools. There might even be a man trap . . .

As he lurked in the lane the caravan door opened and three small children sidled out to inspect him. They were pale-faced and doughy-looking, overweight and squat, a bit like puddings. They stared at Oliver, all in a row, like a set of small toby jugs.

But he wasn't going to be put off by three little kids. In the long grass he could see something quite promising, a cruel-looking cutting instrument with spikes. He bent down to look at it but the Puddings never took their gaze off him. They followed every move he made with their hard little eyes. Then one of them yelled, "Mam! *Mam!*" and a face popped out from the doorway. "Keep your hands off that!" the woman shrieked. "This is private property. So clear off!"

Oliver grabbed his thermos flask and fled, hardly daring to look up at the cheerless farmhouse where the Edges lived, and he didn't stop running till he was outside Miss Brierley's door, at Blake's End.

Nobody answered his knock, so he just walked in. The old lady's bed was in a corner under the window. She lay propped up on pillows but her eyes were shut, and her breathing was irregular and noisy. Rose Salt sat on a chair by the bed, reading slowly and carefully from a copy of *The Times*.

Oliver felt rather ashamed. She *could* read then, and with some expression and feeling. "Rose," he whispered. "I've brought the soup from Molly. You left it behind." Her sad brown eyes slid from the newsprint to the red flask, then to his face. She said nothing, only shook her head slightly, and went on reading. *The Times* was obviously Miss Brierley's bedtime story. She was dozing off quite nicely now, and Rose was pleased.

Oliver walked slowly down the hill again, towards Blake's Pit. The old woman was dying, he'd realised that the minute he entered the house. It wasn't the smell, or the harsh breathing, or the papery chalk-white cheeks, or the lifeless hair. It was something in the air. Death waiting.

It didn't worry him. Several of his mother's old people had been carted off to hospital and never brought back. In time, others, equally old, had replaced them. That was life. But a death like this would upset Prill. She was a touchy, nervous kind of person, with too much imagination for her own good. Oliver hoped the old woman would hang on for a bit longer, at least till they all went home.

Her cottage was in a prime spot, with a perfect view of Blake's Pit down below. Oliver hadn't realised it was quite so big, and he'd forgotten how round it was. The still waters looked very broody and dark today; there was no sun, and rain was threatening. Black Pit was its original name, according to his father, and the locals said it was bottomless.

He shivered slightly, turned up his collar and headed for Elphins. He didn't see the three twisted little faces peering at him through the dirty caravan window, or Sid and Violet Edge spying down on him from their upstairs landing, cracking jokes about his skinny little legs.

Prill had got up very late and spent the morning writing a letter to Angela Stringer. On their way up to Winnie Webster's bungalow she dropped it in the letter box outside the Edges' shop.

"Dear Angela," she'd written. "We're here, and guess what? I've won second prize in a competition. First prize—two weeks' holiday in Stang, Second prize—*three* weeks' holiday in Stang. Ha Ha, funny joke. Do you get the message? It's awful. We're all freezing to death in this house. Molly Bover's quite nice, arty, but definitely rather vague, and forgets half you say. Someone lives in called Rose Salt. She cooks and cleans up, and looks a real weirdo. I should think she's got no parents—Molly's the sort of person who seems to like helping 'lame dogs'.

And while I'm on the subject, she's got these two horrible poodles called Potty and Dotty. Last Christmas someone left them behind, in an empty house, and Molly saved them from the vet's needle! They obviously get on her nerves, but she felt sorry for them. 'One of life's nice people', as your dad would say.

Everyone round here is either old or peculiar, or both. There's a vile family called Edge that seems to rule the village and has a finger in every pie. Nobody

30

likes them, not even Molly. Their Tony (18) is the local heart-throb. Honestly, you should just *see* him.

I *am* going riding by the way, Molly's said she can fix it up for me. There are some horses in the village, three in a field just outside my bedroom window. But guess what? On closer inspection the one I really fancied turned out to be an old carthorse!

Now don't forget to write.

In deepest gloom, Prill."

It really was a masterpiece of spite, and Prill put it in the letter box feeling rather uncomfortable. She hoped the Reverend Stringer wouldn't read it too. If he did, he'd probably drop straight on to his knees and start praying for her soul.

# Chapter Four

Winnie Webster must have been lying in wait for them behind her front door, because the minute they knocked it opened quickly and they were ushered inside. She talked non-stop as she drew up chairs and made them sit down in a small, crowded room. Jessie, curiously cowed by the atmosphere, came in rather unwillingly and slumped at Prill's feet. But the minute she wagged her tail all the ornaments on the mantelpiece rattled.

"Oh dear," Miss Webster said doubtfully. "I didn't know you had a dog. I'm a cat person myself. Do you think—"

"I'll take her outside," Colin said abruptly, getting up. Nobody wanted Jessie in Stang; even Molly had forgotten she was coming. He felt rather depressed as he knotted her lead round the bars of the garden gate, and the odd cooking smells that issued from Winnie's kitchen didn't do much to cheer him up. Molly had warned them that she was rather keen on "health" foods, and it was hours since breakfast.

She gave them all a "pre-lunch" drink, with hard seeds in the bottom and what looked like dead leaves floating about on top. "Cinnamon" she explained crisply, watching Prill trying to fish her bits out. "Nothing added. All freshly squeezed. Drink up now, lunch in twenty minutes."

The three children swallowed the strange brew obediently. Winnie Webster was like that, very small, but with a hard steel core, bustling and energetic—a little human dynamo. She was also a mad keen gardener. Outside the window a plump young man in jeans was scratching his head over an obstinate lawn mower. "That's

Porky Bover," she explained. "No, no relation to Molly, except way back. He's my right hand in this great garden. A marvellous worker. Now then, let's have a chat."

But all they did was listen. Oliver had Winnie Webster taped in about two minutes. Women like her were always coming to see his mother. She was a Committee Lady. She went on and on about church fêtes, and Christmas bazaars, and children's pantomimes. Her life blood was in all this, now she'd retired from school teaching. But what she most wanted to talk about was the play. "You do know about it, of course?" she said, pausing only to draw breath before rushing on.

"Sort of," said Colin, though all Molly had told them was that some of the men and boys in the village put a play on at Easter time. It was very ancient, something to do with St George and a lot of other knights. There was a great deal of fighting in it, but everyone made friends at the end. The dead men came back to life, and they all danced round together.

"*King* George actually," corrected Winnie. "But yes, he's a saint, of course. My dears, you wouldn't *believe* the trouble I have every year with Stang Mummers."

"*Mummers*?" Prill repeated. "Aren't there any words?"

"Oh yes, pretty crude and simple they are too, like nursery rhymes really. But people still have trouble learning their lines, and of course the Edges are quite *hopeless*."

"But I thought mumming meant miming?" Oliver said cleverly.

"Oh it does, and you'd expect it to be performed in silence, I know, Pity it's not, I wouldn't have quite so many problems then."

"So who's in the play?"

"Just the three old village families, the Wrights, the Bovers and the Edges, worst luck, and only the men. Women can't take part. Porky's always in it, he does the

33

women. Oh, he doesn't mind, he's one of the more sensible members of the cast. Pity the others don't copy."

"I'd quite like to read it," Oliver said. His father hadn't told him much about this, and it sounded interesting. "Have you got a copy of the words?"

Winnie Webster hesitated. "Ye-es," she said slowly. "But I can't let you borrow it, I'm afraid."

"Why not?"

A dark pink flush was creeping slowly over her cheeks. She looked distinctly uncomfortable. "Well, it's silly really, but there are a lot of funny customs connected with this play. It's been done for so many years, you see. Certain families always take certain parts, and everything's got to happen in exactly the same way. One of the things they insist on is that only the players have the words. They think it's bad luck if an outsider sees them, or a woman."

"But you're a woman," Oliver said rudely. He was now determined to get his hands on it.

She laughed. "True, but I'm the producer, dear. If I wasn't around they'd end up fighting. Anything that involves the Edge family is always impossible to organize. They're so *difficult*, I just can't tell you. And this year we've got another problem, we've no King George."

She took a framed photograph down from the mantelpiece. "Dear Noel," she murmured. "This is my nephew, Noel Wright. He's a very distant cousin of yours, Oliver. Noel usually plays George, and he's a splendid actor. But this year his company decided to send him to America for six months. Well, of course he couldn't turn that down, not even for Stang Mummers, so I've asked young Mr Massey to do it."

They all looked dutifully at the photograph. "Dear Noel" was a chinless wonder, with piggy little eyes, a spotted bow tie, and sleek hair parted down the middle. George Massey, a T.V. producer, who'd recently moved into a brand-new house opposite Elphins, just had to be

34

an improvement. He'd waved to the children that morning as they came out of Molly's gate, a big man, with a bushy blond beard, and a red T-shirt that said "Ranswick Thespians". He was a very keen amateur actor.

"It should be a Wright really," Winnie explained. "That's what they're all grumbling about. But no one will allow me to swap the parts round, or anything. They say it will 'break the luck', or some nonsense. Codswallop. So I said, 'Look, it's George Massey or nothing.' And they took it, would you believe? His name's George, fortunately, and that seemed to persuade them. Oh, they are *dense*. I did point out that the man's paying for the new costumes this year, so they can't afford to offend him. He's dying to be in it, and he's *very* good."

Prill wasn't at all sure she liked the sound of this play, with all this secrecy about the words, all this talk about "bad luck", the fact that women couldn't be in it, and all the squabbling. "It doesn't sound very Christian to me," she said suddenly.

"Oh well, it's not dear, anything but. All the religious bits have been stuck on, over the years. It's not really supposed to be done at Easter either, but you wouldn't expect Stang people to get a thing like that right, would you? Yes, the whole thing's pagan really, and when you think how they make the horse's head . . ."

"Yes, tell us about that," Oliver said excitedly. It was in his book.

Winnie Webster looked at the three young faces, and paused. It was a bit gruesome, but today's children seemed to like grisly things. "*Well*," she began. "In the play the horse is called Old Hob, and they carry it round on a pole. It's very important, the one thing they always keep. All the other props and costumes are replaced every seven years. Very wasteful I call it, but there you are. The old things are burned on a bonfire—just an excuse for a knees-up, in my opinion. It's tonight actually. Did Molly mention it?"

"No," Colin said. It sounded rather interesting. Perhaps they could go.

"Anyway, everything's burned except this horse's head. It's a real one, boiled down and skinned. They fix wires to its jawbone and someone hides under a cloth and goes round snapping at the audience. The children adore it. Now that really *is* pre-Christian," she said, looking at the girl. "It goes right back to horse worship, that does."

Prill was feeling quite sick. She had just refused to think about a crowd of drunken villagers boiling a poor horse's head in a great pot. Horses were marvellous creatures, there was a great dignity and peace about them. She could quite understand why, in ancient times, men had bowed down and worshipped them like gods.

"In the old days villages used to steal each other's heads, apparently," Winnie said dryly. "It was like robbing them of their magic power, you see. Just the kind of thing the Edge family would adore, I've no doubt," she added, with a queer little laugh. But Prill had gone green.

"Fresh air," Winnie announced briskly, realizing she'd said too much. "I'll just put the spinach on, then we'll go round the garden for five minutes."

*Spinach.* Prill felt even worse.

The real inspection of the garden was postponed till after lunch. The meal was such a strange mixture of flavours, and involved so much hard chewing, that they all felt relieved to be out of the stuffy dining room and walking about in the fresh air. Porky Bover was still having trouble with his lawn mower, and he kept stopping to adjust it. The steeply sloping lawns didn't make the grass very easy to cut, and Oliver couldn't understand why he was doing it anyway. The turf hadn't started to grow again yet, it was obviously taking its time. But then, it was so cold in Stang.

"Can't seem to get the hang of this new mower, Miss Webster," the fat boy shouted good-naturedly, as she led an expedition up the hill to look at the view. "It keeps stopping."

"Well, it was you who complained about the old one, dear," she called rather heartlessly. "Thought this was our answer. All these bits of lawn. All these slopes. Now, would your mother like some bedding plants when they're ready? I'll have plenty of spares."

"You've got a good view of the lake, Miss Webster," Oliver said politely. "As good as Miss Brierley's."

"A wee bit better if anything," she said proudly. "No trees in the way on my side. Some people find it a bit depressing—Molly, for example. Now she wouldn't give tuppence for this view. I just can't persuade her to live down here. She doesn't really like Blake's Pit."

"Why not?" Prill asked.

"Oh, that's Molly; she's a bit of a Romantic, you know. There's supposed to be quite a big town at the bottom of it. Well, a city really. Someone did something terribly wicked once, and someone else put a curse on them, and in the middle of the night a flood rose up from nowhere and drowned everybody."

"What a fantastic story," thought Prill.

"Of course, if dear Molly knew her *geography* and her *geology* Winnie went on, a little peevishly, "she'd know that it couldn't possibly be true." And she delivered a short lecture about earth-mass, glaciers, and rock formations. She was almost as boring as Uncle Stanley.

Tea was threatened, but they were saved from it by Violet Edge who came wandering up the garden with some books under her arm. "Our Vi," Winnie muttered under her breath. "Heavens, it's nearly four o'clock. I'm supposed to be giving her an English lesson. O Level. A lost cause of course, but there we are. Come on, Violet," she shouted down the slope. "My visitors are just leaving. Uncanny resemblance isn't there?" she

37

whispered in Colin's ear, noticing his eyes fixed on Our Vi.

There was. The flat pasty face was that of a fifteen-year-old girl, but she had that same hard look, sullen and suspicious, and those awful burning eyes.

Just as they were going through the front gate Winnie came running out with a book in her hand. She was feeling guilty about snubbing Oliver. He'd been so interested in the play, and you really should encourage bright children, not fob them off with talk of old superstitions.

"Oliver," she said. "You might like to read this. It's not the *text* of the play, but it *is* quoted quite a lot."

He took the small blue book, and read the title: *The Stang Mumming Play, Origins and History*. It was by Winifred B. Webster B.A. (Hons), Manchester. "*Thank you*," he beamed, rather impressed. "I'll read it, and bring it straight back."

"No, that's all right. But do look after it, Oliver. In fact, I'm not quite sure really . . ." and she put her hand out, almost as if she was going to snatch it back again.

"Why shouldn't I read it?" Oliver said, hardening.

Winnie Webster said nothing for a minute, then she became cheerful and brisk again. But there was something forced in her manner now. "Well, *quite*. *Why* shouldn't you? All this superstitious nonsense, all this secrecy. It's ridiculous. Keep it at Molly's though, dear, don't take it round the village." *Don't let the Edges see you with it* was what she really meant.

Our Vi didn't hear the conversation because the bungalow windows were all shut, but she certainly saw the book change hands, and as she sat waiting for her lesson an unpleasant smile was spreading slowly across her flat face.

Oliver tucked the book under his arm and followed Jessie along the lane. He was very thoughtful. Miss Webster's crisp, no-nonsense manner hadn't been at all convincing. It was as if, deep down, she was frightened of something. What on earth was it?

# Chapter Five

There had been no sign of a bonfire when they walked up to Winnie's, but now the lanes were full of scurrying children lugging bits of dead tree up the hill, and rooting about in the hedges for branches and sticks. Rose Salt was there, helping some boys push an old pram full of rubbish. A loud argument was going on in the field next to George Massey's new house; the Edges were building their fire there, and he said it was too close to his fence.

"You've got the whole field," they heard. "Why build it here, for heaven's sake?"

"Whole field's no good," Tony Edge said cheekily. "It's all waterlogged, that's what. This bit's the only place we *can* build it. Any fool can see that."

But George wouldn't be shouted down, and, very grudgingly, they started to dismantle their fire. Sid turned up, with the Puddings in tow, and Our Vi appeared soon afterwards and helped to heave great branches about. The grumpy man who'd yelled at Colin from his bedroom window stood in the gateway and directed operations in a loud, harsh voice. This was Uncle Harold, brother of Uncle Frank. Together they ran the village stores, and they were also the stars of the play, according to Winnie.

"Seen enough?" Sid Edge bawled at Colin, who stood watching outside Molly's. He turned, and walked up the garden path. The Edges weren't doing anything constructive, they were just shifting their wood about six feet from the fence. That was no good. When darkness fell, and George Massey went indoors, he wouldn't put it past them to creep out and move everything back to its original place. They were like that.

"How was Winnie?" Molly Bover asked them at tea. "Did she give you all a carrot juice cocktail?"

Colin and Prill exchanged embarrassed looks, but Oliver said, "Yes, it was awful. And the lunch was pretty awful, too. It tasted most peculiar." He was totally unpredictable. In some moods he was maddeningly polite to grownups, at other times he said exactly what he thought. Aunt Phyllis wouldn't approve, but Oliver was clearly enjoying a little taste of freedom.

Molly grinned. "Good old Winnie. I expect you're all genned up now. I expect she gave you her lecture about Stang, and the play, and old Cheshire customs. Am I right?"

"Well, *yes*," Oliver said slowly. "But I'm still not sure about Blake's Pit."

"What about it, dear?"

"She said it was supposed to have a town at the bottom, and that there was a curse on it. She said you knew all about it too, but that it was a load of old rubbish," he ended tactlessly.

"Ah yes," Molly said quietly. "Winnie rather likes that word. She just means an old poem, I think, one I'm rather fond of:

*He has cursed aloud that city proud,*
*He has cursed it in its pride;*
*He has cursed it into Semmerwater*
*Down the brant hillside;*
*He has cursed it into Semmerwater,*
*There to bide . . ."*

Her voice was rich and deep, like a great river. What a pity women couldn't be in this play, Prill thought. Molly would be marvellous.

Oliver had listened very carefully. "*Semmerwater*," he said accusingly. "But what's that got to do with it? It's in Yorkshire. I've been. My father took me rowing on it."

"Full marks, Oliver," Molly said patiently, thinking that the persistent, pernickety Oliver was rather like a dentist's drill. "But there are legends like that about lots of places, you know, with little variations. Didn't your father tell you?"

"No. He's not very keen on poetry."

"Well, in the poem, a beggar is turned away from the gates of a great city, and he curses it. And the floods rise and drown everyone."

"Yes, she told us *that*," he said impatiently.

And did she tell you that people have actually *seen* the city, shimmering through the water?"

"No, no she didn't. I don't think she likes poetry much either."

"Ah well," said Molly.

*"King's tower and queen's bower,*
*And a mickle town and tall;*
*By glimmer of scale and gleam of fin*
*Folks have seen them all . . ."*

The sheer music of it made Prill's spine tingle. What a pity Molly Bover didn't take them for poetry lessons. Their English teacher, old Mr Crockford, read things like that to them with all the feeling of an iron bar. "What about Stang, Molly?" she said.

"Well, nobody's ever bothered to write a poem about Blake's Pit, but it's got the same kind of story attached to it, only in our version it was only the rich people who drowned. The beggar survived and prospered, and built another town by the lake. That's one explanation of why Stang village is where it is. Old Stang's under the water, and the oldest houses are just above it."

"But I thought this house was the oldest in the village?" Oliver said.

"Oh no, dear, Pit Farm's the oldest, and it's the third house on that sight, apparently. The Edges do go back a

41

very long way, and I suppose when your name's in Doomsday Book you can afford to feel a bit superior."

"They are *awful* though, Molly," Colin said fiercely, thinking of Rose Salt weeping over her smashed eggs, and of Sid's peals of laughter.

"Yes, they are. Sometimes, though, I get the feeling that wretched family just can't help itself. They were *born* awkward, somehow."

"Perhaps it was one of the Edges who cursed that palace into the pit," Oliver said solemnly. "Perhaps they're all descended from that old beggar."

"They claim to be, as a matter of fact," Molly murmured. "It's a local tradition. No way of proving it, of course, but the Edges are quite proud of their ancestry. Most people would keep quiet about it, if someone way back had been responsible for a curse, but not that lot . . . *Now*," she said briskly. "If you're going to this bonfire, wrap up well—and keep an eye on Rose for me. She gets rather excited on these occasions."

What she meant was that Rose Salt had a crush on Tony Edge. They could see her, standing in the shadows, peeping at Uncle Harold as he poured petrol on the bonfire. She was still wearing her woolly pixie-hood and the long brown mack, and clinging on to her old shopping bag. Tony was surrounded by a group of giggling admirers. They watched him fit a big harness on to his shoulders, then slot a long pole into it, down a leather pouch, rather like a boy scout carrying a flag. Then he began to sway about, laughing and chasing after all the girls. The bonfire had blazed up already, and in the orange glare Prill saw the outline of a horse's skull.

"Old Hob, Old Hob, Give him a tanner, Give him a bob," Tony was shouting, and lurching round the field, careering up to little knots of people who stood warming themselves at the fire. Oliver was fascinated by the horse, and stuck very close to it as Tony charged about, but it was too spooky for Prill.

The huge, grinning skull, hung with tattered ribbons, waved and dipped in the flickering light, and bonfire sparks showered up over it like gold rain. "Come on, Posie," she whispered, skirting round the edge of the bonfire to avoid Tony and his horrible horse. "Your dad's brought some sausages out. Should we have one?" Prill had acquired a little friend, George Massey's two-year-old daughter. They had seen her that afternoon "helping" her father in the garden, and Prill had crossed the road to say hello.

She was the complete opposite of their small sister. Alison was solid and dark, with a red face, and charged about in a state of perpetual stickiness. This child was doll-like and fragile-looking, with a mass of curly blonde hair. Colin had christened her Goldilocks. Her mother Brenda was at home, trying to get Posie's six-month-old brother Sam to sleep. Prill was only too delighted to look after her while George Massey carried food round on trays.

The Edges weren't at all grateful. "It's not Bonfire Night, y'know," someone grumbled, inspecting a baked potato, then putting it back. "We don't normally have food. Any road, it's burnt this is." But the Puddings were out in force, all standing in a line and staring into the flames, the fierce light splashing their intense little faces. They grabbed all that was offered, sausages, potatoes. ginger parkin, and gobbled away in silence. "I don't know," George Massey muttered to the Blakemans. "There's no pleasing some people. They might say thank you."

After about ten minutes the two butcher brothers dragged an old hamper up to the fire and opened the lid. From all over the field dark shadows flocked to it, like wasps to a jampot. Tony left Old Hob in the grass and shoved his way to the front. "Clear off, Rose Salt," they

43

heard. But the adoring little figure still trailed after him, keeping her distance, in the darkness.

Before the costumes were thrown on the fire people put them on and tore round noisily. There was a definite excitement in the air now; this was obviously much more important than spuds and sausages. George Massey was rather surprised. "I didn't know this went on," he said, watching faceless shapes struggle into flopping garments.

Winnie had told them that the Stang Mummers' costumes were rather special, very brightly coloured, and each one decorated with a special emblem to tell you who it was. On "the night" all players wore hoods that fell over their faces.

In the dark everything was reduced to a black silhouette, and there was a lot of pushing and shouting. They watched two figures fight over something and eventually tear it in two. Then, quite suddenly, the bobbing shapes separated out like a line of paper men, and went dancing crazily round the bonfire, hand in hand.

"I want to, I want to," grizzled Posie Massey. She liked dressing up. Her father was feeling rather peeved. His wife had gone to all this trouble with the food, and they'd treated him like dirt. It was his field anyway, the Edges only rented it, and the bonfire was much too close to his fence. They couldn't do anything properly.

"All right, kid," he said. "Let's find you something pretty. Don't see why those boys should have all the fun, do you?"

"And I want ma horse," the child whimpered. Posie Massey had a new playroom full of toys, and pride of her collection was a painted hobby horse on a wooden stick. She'd heard there was a horse at the bonfire and she'd brought hers.

It was a night for horses. As they went over to the hamper, Prill heard whinnying in the field by Elphins. Did fire frighten horses, she wondered, or did they warm themselves against the flames, like great cats? She thought of the three horses in the field below her window, Mister and Lucky Lady, the two chestnuts, and William, the lame old carthorse. What had those peaceful creatures to do with this devilish dancing, with these hateful, snapping jaws? Prill longed to be clopping down a quiet country lane on old William's back, far away from the Edges, Stang, and that brooding pit in the valley bottom.

In helping to dress Posie, and getting her astride her tiny horse, George Massey made his first mistake. "Old Hob, Old Hob," the child chanted in a little squeaky voice, and went tottering off towards the bonfire where the faceless black dancers were wriggling out of their costumes, rolling them into balls, and hurling them into the fire with hoarse shouts and squeals.

Everything happened very quickly after that. A hand shot out of the shadows and stopped the child in its tracks; in seconds she was surrounded by thrusting figures, a yelling, jostling scrum, all trying to grab the pathetic little prize. She screamed, and a voice said, "You can't wear that, chuck. Off with it, come on. Got to go on the fire, that has." Then another voice broke in, a girl's, hard and peevish. "It's not fair, any road. Girls can't be in this. Give it me, will you. I'll throw it on. Ouch! *Give over!*"

Costume, mask and hood were torn off the terrified toddler and thrown into the leaping flames, and the toy horse followed. With mirthless shrieks the dancers melted away into the dark, and Posie Massey was left alone on the grass, sobbing for her mother, and with Prill down on her knees, trying to comfort her.

George Massey suddenly saw red. He left Prill and Posie together and stormed off. In less than a minute he was back at the bonfire with something held high above his head. It was Old Hob.

Afterwards he swore that he thought it was part of the custom, that the horse was burned too, along with everything else, but nobody ever believed him. George simply wanted to take part in his own bonfire. They'd laughed at his food, hurt his child, and ignored his instructions about the fence. Nothing was left to burn now, except this great grinning puppet on a stick.

He was a tall man. With one heave he raised the thing right above his shoulders like a dumb-bell, twirled it round twice, then hurled it into the heart of the fire. Tony Edge let out a scream, then he went mad. Gibbering like an idiot he looked round wildly, then he ran to the gate and pulled something out of the grass, an old ladder they'd used to build the bonfire.

"Leave off, Tone!" someone shouted, but he was almost weeping with rage. He dragged his ladder to the fire and managed to lift it up on his own. The children stared, hypnotized, amazed at his brute strength. He was actually trying to crawl along it. "We'll save him," he was bellowing. "We've got to save him." His voice was half a scream, half a sob, and for one crazy moment Prill felt quite sorry for him.

But the uncles had taken over and were pulling him back. "Don't be stupid, Tone! Leave off, will you!" Then—"*Look at the fire, man!*" No one had been watching it, and the weight of the ladder had made it slump over towards the freshly creosoted fence. Slowly the bonfire fell to pieces, there was no heart to it and it was shoddily built, like everything the Edges had a hand in. The crowd gasped and George Massey shouted hoarsely "I *knew* it. I *knew* something like this would happen." The fence was alight already, and the flames were spreading right along. It was like watching the fuse go up on a huge firework.

There were buckets of water lined up behind the fence. George had made his preparations, he wasn't born yesterday. He bellowed instructions to Harold and Frank Edge, then tore off to dial 999. Then he got into his brand-new car and backed it down his drive. Thank heaven my insurance is in order, he was thinking, as he ran back to the field. Let's hope I won't need it.

But he hadn't reckoned with the wind. It was sucking burning brands out of the fire and hurling them into the air. One of them landed on the garage roof, and it was timber. He rang the fire brigade again and told them things were getting out of hand. "Don't worry, sir," a calm country voice said on the end of the phone. "They're on their way. They'll be with you in five minutes."

Oliver, Colin and Prill were told to keep out of the way, with Posie. They stood back and watched, but it was no good telling the Edges what to do. They were all trying to help with the chain of buckets, but there were so many of them and it was so dark. All they succeeded in doing was wreaking havoc. Several buckets got spilt, a child was burned when something fell out of the fire, and Prill heard Sid arguing with his sister about who should help Uncle Frank as he beat at the flattened embers with a broom.

"Sometimes I think that family can't help it." Molly's words came back to Colin, as he watched their hopeless efforts. Were they really trying to help George Massey? Or were they deliberately being stupid? Half of him suspected that they were quite enjoying themselves, almost willing everything to go up in flames.

The first call had been answered immediately, and an engine had been dispatched to Stang within minutes, tearing with screaming sirens down the misty April lanes. It wasn't an easy village to find, but one man on board knew this part of Cheshire like the back of his hand and he guided them.

But somehow the driver kept missing his way. Two miles out of Ranswick they got lost in a tangle of roads and had to turn back. Then they reached a dead end. "Road Up" one sign said, and another, "Road Closed, Due to Flooding". The chief fireman was getting frantic because calls kept coming through on his radio. Where were they? Couldn't they hurry up? Couldn't honest ratepayers expect more than this from an emergency call? Were they making their wills?

47

"This is beyond me," the man at the wheel said dumbly, turning round yet again and tearing back up a hill. "It's just like the war. It's like the day they took all the signposts away because of Jerry."

It took them a good half-hour to find Stang, and when they arrived it was all over. The fence was gone, George Massey's new double garage was a charred ruin, and his wife Brenda was weeping quietly at the kitchen table.

# Chapter Six

If the Edges were hoping that George Massey would pack his bags and go, they must have been very disappointed the next morning. Colin could see him out of the bedroom window, clearing up last night's debris quite cheerfully. It would take more than a fire to shift *him*. He'd never been happy with that garage anyway and he was already planning a new one, with a games-room on top.

Winnie Webster pedalled past on her bicycle and Colin heard them discussing the new costumes. "I've ordered the material," she was saying to George, "and I'm going into Ranswick later to collect it . But *surely*, now . . ."

"Don't let's discuss it out here, Winnie. Get them to send me the bill, as we agreed. See you at tonight's rehearsal," he called after her, as if nothing had happened.

Colin got dressed and took Jessie out for a walk. Sid was lolling against Edge Brothers' shop window, and inside Tony was serving someone with sausages. "Why aren't you at school, Sid?" said Winnie. "You've not broken up yet, have you?"

The boy gave a big sniff. "Coldansorethroat, miss," he said, wiping his nose on his sleeve.

"Use your *handkerchief*, Sid. I suppose that means you'll miss the rehearsal?"

"Oh no, miss," he replied, with another almighty sniff.

"Go home to bed then," she flung tartly over her shoulder, and pedalled away.

Colin walked up the gloomy lane to Stang church. There was a feeble sun shining, but it didn't feel much warmer. He might join the others in Molly's studio when he got back; she was showing them how to throw pots. It was always warm in there, even when the kiln wasn't on; the thick old walls obviously retained the heat. The poodles had discovered that too, and Dotty kept disappearing. Yesterday Molly had found her nesting in a box of jumble she'd left in there for the next church fête, and she was always climbing into drawers and hiding. Dotty was a good name for her, she had a screw loose.

All the way to the church Colin kept stopping and looking round. He felt he was being followed. It was nothing he could see or hear, the only sound was his feet squelching through last year's leaves; there was nothing but the damp, dripping lane, and the trees that clasped leafless hands over his head, stealing the light.

He let Jessie off the lead and she went romping ahead and out of sight. The churchyard was very quiet. He looked round for the builders, but there was no sign of them. No sign either of whoever had followed him up the lane. No one there but the dead. He walked over to the bottom of the tower and peered up through the scaffolding. If he was going to be an archaeologist he'd have to get used to clambering about on old buildings. Anyway, he wasn't chicken. Not like Oliver, who didn't even like using lifts.

He left Jessie snuffling about in the long grass and cautiously made his way up the first ladder to the top of the square tower. But he knew he couldn't climb an inch higher. Over his head the thin steeple was bending horribly. Colin simply couldn't look at it. Nausea and dizziness swept over him like a cold sea, and he made his way down again, blindly this time, hardly daring to open his eyes.

Back on the level he sat down on a flat gravestone and wiped the sweat from his face. He felt so sick he couldn't raise his face again to look at that awful tower. Then he heard something, a sliding, grinding noise from up above, and a loud rattling, as if someone was working ropes and pulleys. Everything started to move at once. The noises grew louder and louder, all merging together in one massive wave of sound, powerful enough to split an eardrum. The steeple was falling.

"No, *no*," he moaned, shaking his head wildly from side to side. But through closed eyes he could see everything, the crooked finger beckoning, lurching sideways, then crashing down and disappearing into huge clouds of rubble and dust, turning the enormous churchyard trees to matchwood. As it fell, the Edges, Wrights and Bovers leaped from their graves and ran shrieking down the sodden lane towards Blake's Pit.

Colin screamed and forced his eyelids open. A black shower of rooks flew up into the sky, but the tower, with its leaning steeple, was perfectly still. The builders' tarpaulins flapped gently in the wind and in the grass at his feet lay Jessie. She was trying to bark but only made a pathetic little sound, like the mewing of a kitten, and one of her shaggy front paws had disappeared under a large piece of newly cut stone.

He took her back to Elphins in the builder's barrow. She was a heavy dog to lift, but he rolled her in somehow and set off. She didn't struggle, or try to bite him, she just lay there in a heap, uttering dry little yelping sounds. Colin loved this dog. Rage and hatred welled up inside him towards whoever had done such a thing, but as he manoeuvred the barrow over the potholes his hot passions ebbed away, leaving him cold and numb. That stone hadn't been aimed at Jessie at all; it had been meant for him.

He tried to keep his eyes away from the sticky pink-and-white pulp that was the dog's left paw. Her whole leg might be broken, and she might limp for ever. What use would that be to a creature like this? Colin couldn't bear it. As he thought of her tearing across the fields on their long country walks at home, his eyes filled with tears. She'd be better dead.

Who was responsible? His first thought was Sid Edge, but that was impossible. He'd climbed up the church tower as far as the base of the steeple, and seen the tiny platform constructed for the two stonemasons. There was no way Sid could have got up there without Colin seeing him, unless he'd climbed up from the other side, and he wasn't Spiderman. The lump of sandstone was enormous anyway. How could anyone have heaved that at him with such force?

As he pushed the barrow past the village shop he saw Sid lolling against the window. He looked as though he'd been there all day, and his nose was running like a tap. He said nothing as Colin trudged by, but glanced in the barrow with cold curiosity, and sniffed. No coming forward to see what the matter was, no offer of help. Resisting the temptation to spit in his eye, Colin left Jessie by Molly's car and ran into the house.

When she saw the dog Molly dropped everything. Shouting instructions to Rose about food and walking the poodles, she bundled Prill and Oliver into the car, helped Colin to lift Jessie into the back, then drove to Ranswick at sixty miles an hour.

No one said very much as they hurtled along the twisty lanes. The car was going so fast that they all felt slightly sick. The best thing to do was to look out of the window and let Molly concentrate on the driving, otherwise she might crash. But whenever she had to slow down or stop, she always asked Colin the same question, in a voice that was kind enough but quite firm. "What on earth *happened*, lovie?"

In the end he told a straight lie. He said he'd been clambering about on the pile of stones, and that the whole thing had collapsed and trapped Jessie's paw. "It was my own fault," he added in a small voice, feeling the red flush creeping up over his cheeks. "I—I put them straight again, more or less." He didn't want Molly to start quizzing the builder, the fat would really be in the fire if she did that. But how could he tell her that a great block of sandstone had come hurtling out of the sky, just missing him but crushing Jessie's foot? It sounded ridiculous. He wanted to talk to Prill about it, and Oliver, if he was in the right mood. *First the fire, and then the steeple*. It was like a line from one of Molly's old poems.

In less than ten minutes they were outside the vet's surgery. It belonged to an old friend of Molly's, Jimmy Bostock. Oliver got out of the car feeling most peculiar, his heaving stomach almost turned inside out. *Pets*, he thought grimly. He really could manage without them. All this fuss about a dog. Honestly, it was only her paw; he just couldn't understand why everyone was so upset. It was Colin's fault anyway, building sites were always dangerous. He should never have taken the dog near the church.

The vet asked Colin to bring the dog into his consulting room, but Prill pulled him back. "Let Molly do it," she said in a wobbly voice, and she slumped down on a chair, clutching his arm. The smell of antiseptic wafting through the open door, and the thought of all those bright, sharp instruments had made her feel horribly queasy. She was sensible in every other way, but she just couldn't stand the sight of blood, and it was always quite a performance getting her to go to the dentist's. Needles and drills did funny things to Prill; she only had to look at them and she keeled over.

"Look, I'll stay out here," Colin whispered to Molly. "She just might pass out if she goes in there." So the three of them sat in a row, the brother and sister staring at the closed inner door, trying not to think of what might be happening to Jessie, Oliver bored and slightly irritated, flicking through old copies of *Cheshire Life*.

The vet was very reassuring. He came out of his surgery after about twenty minutes and told them the foot looked very much worse than it was. "The leg may well be fractured," he explained, "but let's hope it's a clean break. And the paw's O.K. We've cleaned up the mess, and it's all fairly superficial. She's a lucky dog."

"Can we see her?" Prill said.

"No. I've given her an injection. Ring tomorrow at nine o'clock. Jackie'll be here if I'm not, and she'll put you in the picture." Jackie Bostock was Jimmy's daughter; she helped in the surgery when she was home from boarding school. She was a plump, fresh-faced girl with a big smile, and horses were the passion of her life.

As Prill climbed back miserably into the car, Molly handed her a bit of paper. "An address dear, from Jackie. The riding school near Saltersly Cross. We can give them a ring when we get home. Cheer up, just think—if Jessie hadn't had this little accident we'd never have got that. My memory's like a sieve these days. All things work together for good, Prill."

"*To those that love God*," Oliver piped up priggishly from behind. "That's the important bit." Aunt Phyllis sometimes made him learn pieces of the Bible off by heart.

If she'd not been driving, Molly would have turned round and clobbered him, and Prill cried nearly all the way home. She didn't believe the vet. They sometimes put animals to sleep and told you when it was all over. How could Oliver be so thick-skinned? Colin felt like hitting him, too. And as for everything "working together for good", what did that mean? There was something very wrong in Stang. It was something to do with the Edge family. And he felt that what had happened in the last twenty-four hours was only the beginning.

That night the Mummers met in the old schoolroom for their first play rehearsal, and the three children went over to watch. There were a few dirty looks when Molly brought them to the door and Winnie found a bench for them to sit on, but the two women took no notice. "They

54

need a bit of cheering up," Prill heard. "Missing home, I suspect, and the dog's at the vet's . . ."

They weren't the only spectators anyway. Quite a few small children were sliding around the floor, and some old villagers stood chatting at the back, waiting for Winnie to start. Rose Salt was there too, hovering by the exit.

Oliver decided that all this fuss about keeping the words a secret was pure nonsense. Why go on about secrecy, if people were allowed to come to rehearsals? The Edges couldn't think for themselves. All they knew was that people had done things privately way back, and behind locked doors. It wasn't like that nowadays, and without Winnie Webster there wouldn't be a play at all. He had no qualms about picking something up off the floor and sliding it into his back pocket. It was a spare copy of the words which someone had dropped on the way in. It just might come in useful.

The rehearsal was a shambles. Half the actors hadn't learned their lines, the others hadn't brought their parts, and to start the proceedings Sid's young cousin Samantha, from the caravan, wet her pants and began to wail. With lightning speed Winnie produced a spare pair from her large brown handbag. "Church jumble," she whispered to Prill. "Invaluable. Now come on, Samantha, just pop outside with Vi and slip them on, then we can get going . . ."

Porky Bover started the play off, sweeping an imaginary circle on the floor with an old brush. "Room, Room, Gallons of Room," he said clearly, then:

"*My masters sent me here some room for to provide.*
*So therefore, gentle dears, stand back on every side.*"

"Good, Porky. Now then, where are the devils? Come on Jack, Sid, your turn next. Make a really bold entry, you've got to scare everybody."

Oliver was at his worst. He'd already read Winnie's

book on the Stang play, and he kept lecturing the others about what was going on. "That circle on the floor is very important," he whispered. "It's magic, you see. It's like a fairy ring. Nobody can cross it."

"Oh, belt up!" Colin snapped. "We're trying to listen."

But there wasn't much to listen to. Sid and his father played the devils, and Jack Edge certainly looked the part. He was just a hairier version of his sons, thirty years on, with a huge, dark beard. But he couldn't remember his lines. "The man's an idiot," Oliver said to himself. "They're so *simple*, like jingles."

"Oh, come on Jack," Winnie said impatiently. "Here, *read* them."

"*In come I, Old Beelzebub,*
*Over my shoulder I carries my club,*
*In my hand a dripping pan.*
*Don't you think I'm a jolly old man?*"

He delivered his four lines in a loud, flat voice, and he looked anything but jolly; the great beard made him look rather sinister, with the hard Edge face brooding over it. Sid's acting skills didn't come from his father. He skipped through his lines quite easily:

"*In come I, little Devil Doubt,*
*If you don't give me money*
*I'll sweep you all out.*"

When he said the last bit he grabbed Porky's broom and thrust it at the audience, across the fairy ring.

"*Excellent*," Winnie said, rather surprised. Sid was very good. It was a pity he couldn't have a slightly bigger part.

The children could see why George Massey wasn't very popular. He was rather too professional. He had quite a lot to say, and he delivered his lines with gusto, in an enormous voice.

*"In comes I, King George,*
*King George that valiant man with courage bold.*
*Twas I that won five crowns of gold,*
*Twas I that fought the fiery dragon and brought him*
*to a slaughter*
*And by that fight I hope to win*
*The Queen of Egypt's daughter."*

"Marvellous, George," Winnie beamed enthusiastically when he'd been through his part. But there were jealous scowls all round, and when he started interfering the Edges looked murderous. "Can't we liven it up a bit?" he suggested. "It's all a bit flat, I think. When Harold enters, for example, couldn't he say something like, 'You can't get *this* on the National Health', say, when he takes his magic potion out? That'd raise a few laughs."

There was a sudden silence in the schoolroom. Harold Edge went up to him, and actually grabbed him by the shirt collar. "Look, Massey," he hissed, "I've always played the Doctor and I don't need *you* to tell me what to do, *see*? I play my part, and you play yours. Get it?"

George Massey began to bluster. "Of course, Harold, of course. I understand. I only thought—"

"Only *nothing*" the man snarled. "You're not at the BBC now, you know."

"What Harold means, George, is that, well, all this is very old, you see. It wouldn't be right to add things at this stage. It's not Shakespeare, of course. All the same . . ." Winnie twittered on nervously, but she was on Harold's side in this. It would be quite wrong to put cheap modern jokes into the play.

"Can't we get on, Winnie?" a voice bawled. "Are we going to be here all night?"

Slowly the rehearsal lapsed into chaos. The children tore round, bashing each other with the flat wooden swords provided for the fights, and the Edge brothers got into an argument with Winnie about the horse's head. Old

Hob had been found in the ashes of the bonfire, but the skull was badly charred. Frank said they'd have to borrow a head from the Saltersly Mummers, who performed their play on Christmas Eve.

But Harold looked black when this was suggested. "It's not the same," he grumbled. "It's not the same at all. And if it hadn't been for that fool Massey . . ."

"Oh, be realistic Harold," Winnie interrupted sharply. "*Of course* you'll have to borrow one, and the Saltersly head's splendid. I'm sure they'll lend it."

Before the practice broke up she gave out parcels of material, all neatly labelled. "Take them home," she ordered. "Rope in your mothers, sisters, grannies. Everyone knows the basic pattern, and the sooner they all start cutting and stitching the happier I will be." As they squabbled over the packages, Rose Salt glided forward. "I'll do Slasher's, miss," she whispered. Slasher, the purple knight who fought with King George at the end, was being played by Tony Edge.

"Yes, of course, Rose," beamed Winnie, remembering how well she could sew. Elphins was full of her patchwork cushions and embroidered tablecloths.

Tony Edge didn't like it. "Don't want *her* messing my costume up," he grunted, as Rose slipped away. "Don't be silly, Tony," Winnie snapped. "And don't be so ungrateful. Rose is marvellous with a needle. Count yourself lucky my boy."

Molly was in bed when they got back. "Early night," her note said. "Cocoa on the stove. Sweet dreams, everybody." They sat round the kitchen table talking about the play, then noticed Oliver's photographs in a bag marked "Kwik Flicks, Ranswick".

"It *was* quick," he said, undoing the packet. "Wonder how they've turned out?"

Prill and Colin noticed, with some relief, that Oliver was a rotten photographer. At least there was something he couldn't do. There were a few snaps of their Irish holiday last year, Colin buried in sand, Mum, Dad and Jessie with no heads, one of Prill's knees. Most of the others were of Christmas day at 9, Thames Terrace, with Aunt Phyllis grimly carving a turkey and all the old people in funny hats. Only the last photo on the roll was of Stang. It was the picture Oliver had taken through the car window.

"That was a bit of a waste, Oll," Colin said, yawning. "Why take a picture of a hedge, for heaven's sake? I'm off to bed anyway. Coming up, Prill?" He knew she didn't like climbing those stairs in the dark.

When they'd gone, Oliver had another look at his Stang photograph. He'd got the nest in, but it would have to be enlarged before an expert could make anything of it. He felt rather disappointed. Then, above the hedge, he saw something else, something he'd not noticed when he clicked the shutter, something that hadn't been there. It was a face.

He dropped the picture with a little cry. His fingers felt hot and sore, as if he'd singed them on an iron, and he sat down shaking, with a tingling sensation racing up and down his back. It was as though he'd just touched a bare electric wire.

Then he looked again. It wasn't just the pattern of treeless branches, or strange cloud shapes up in the sky, it was a face that stared out at him, looking him straight in the eyes. Oliver was a bit of a coward, but he grasped the snapshot firmly and stared at the innocent hedge. The face that looked back made him go cold. It was a face stripped of all human feeling, all tenderness, all love. Something in that great hard mouth and those enormous, burning eyes filled the terrified Oliver with a great darkness, and he slumped down on a stool, his knees almost giving way under him.

"Can I have a look?" a little voice said. Rose Salt was standing behind him.

"Yes, yes, of course, Rose," Oliver stammered. "They're not much good though."

When Rose saw the Stang photograph she dropped it quickly, then she pushed it away from her to the other side of the battered table, and they stared at one another in silence.

"Room for improvement, don't you think?" Oliver said at last, with a dry little laugh. But Rose, with her eye on the crumpled photo, was backing away, saying she was going to bed, and the look on her face was one of absolute terror.

# Chapter Seven

As soon as Prill woke up next morning she opened the bedroom window and stuck her head out. It was raining and the field was misty, but she signalled as usual to Lucky Lady, Mister, and old William, and waited for them to come trotting up towards the house. Dad had taught her to whistle through her fingers last year, and it drove Colin mad. He couldn't do it, because of the shape of his teeth. Aunt Phyllis would no doubt say it wasn't "lady like".

The three horses didn't come. The village felt cold and dead, water dripped off the roof on to Prill's head, and the rain poured down monotonously into the murky field. The leafless tree in the far corner where they sometimes stood, whisking their tails, looked like an old beggar woman in the thin light, her knobbled limbs frozen for ever in wild entreaty. The huge oak must be centuries old. Prill stared at its tangled branches. She sometimes saw faces in trees, and in the red of a dying fire, faces that frightened her. She gave one last whistle, listened, then shut the window. Then she pulled her clothes on and went downstairs.

"Where are the horses?" she asked Molly. The kitchen had a rich yeasty smell. Rose Salt had been mixing dough that morning but she was out on one of her mysterious little "errands". Molly was frying eggs and bacon.

"Hello, dear," she said. "You're up early. Have some breakfast." Then, "The *horses*?" she repeated, rather absently.

"You know, the ones outside my bedroom, that lame old carthorse and those two chestnuts," Prill said irritably. Something else was wrong with today, and it was only when she sat down to eat that she remembered what it was. Jessie was at the vet's, and in an hour or so they'd know the worst. The sound of the poodles barking away in the studio made her want to scream.

"I'll just go and have a look in the field again," she said tensely, looking round for her wellingtons. She was pulling them on when Molly said suddenly, "Oh, I remember now, dear. Jack Edge took them up to Big Meadow. Better grazing or something. There's not much doing down here yet, it's been such a wet winter."

"Why did Jack Edge take them?"

"They're his horses. The field's his too."

"Where is Big Meadow?"

"Just out of the village, up Coffin Lane. Quite a nice walk, if it would only stop raining."

Prill was torn. She wanted to go and look for them straight away, but there was Jessie to consider. Molly was phoning Bostocks' at nine, and she ought to be around. She would have to wait till they got back from Ranswick. If it brightened up she could take Posie Massey with her; Brenda had been hinting that the child got bored and bad-tempered with nobody to play with.

Jessie hobbled out of Bostocks' unaided. She was very subdued and her leg and paw were swathed in thick dressings, but at least she was in one piece. When she saw the children she wagged her tail feebly. The vet gave Molly various pills and spare dressings, and also a bill. When she opened it she pulled a face, and the Blakemans exchanged embarrased looks. Dad hadn't been told about the "accident" yet. He wasn't going to be too pleased. But Molly crumpled the bill into her pocket. "Don't worry about it, loves. It can wait. Let's just be grateful the old thing's still with us, eh?"

Oliver was sitting in the front of the car, irritated by the way his cousins were drooling over the dog. All right, so it would always limp, but it seemed chirpy enough to him. "At least it's *alive*," he pointed out. "I mean, it might have been *killed*."

"Oh, shut up, Oliver," Colin said angrily. He'd had enough of these tactless comments; his cousin was too clever by half. "If that's all you can say, I'd keep quiet. And Jessie's a *she*, not an *it*."

"All right, all right, pardon me for living," and Oliver didn't say another word. But when they reached the big roundabout on the edge of the town he asked Molly to stop. "I think I'll go to the library while I'm here," he said, getting out. "There's something I want to look up."

His cousins looked at each other. "*Sulking*," Prill mouthed.

"Oh, let him," Colin muttered as Oliver wrote down Molly's directions about getting to the bus station, in a large notebook.

"What is this 'research' he's doing?" she said, as they drove away.

"Dunno. First we've heard of it," Colin answered.

"Uncle Stanley sometimes gives him projects and things to do in the holidays," Prill explained. "It might be something to do with that." In another mood she'd have felt rather sorry for Oliver, but just at the moment she was mad with him.

Ranswick had a brand new library housed in an ugly concrete building several storeys high. There was only one bus a day to Stang, so time was short. Swallowing his nerves he got into the lift and was catapulted to the top floor. First he went to the enquiry desk and asked for details of the Ranswick and District Natural History Society. The secretary lived a few minutes' walk away from the town centre, so it would be easy to find. He checked that the photograph was still in his back pocket, then went to the "local history" section.

The Blakemans reckoned there was nothing about Stang in the guidebooks, but Oliver knew that you had to do a bit of detective work to get the really interesting information. His cousins didn't stick at anything. He hunted along the shelves and soon found what he wanted. Then he opened his notebook and put his glasses on.

In a book called "*Stang—Portrait of a Village*" he found that Molly's story was quite true. Blake's Pit was described as "dark and brooding", and compared to Wastwater in the Lake District. "Both", the author went on, "have been described as 'the last place that God ever made'." It said that ill luck was supposed to have dogged the people of Stang ever since "that fatal turning away of the beggar at the gates, all those centuries ago", that the survivors of the flood had "lived and died in sorrow", and that the beggar's curse had been passed down, from generation to generation. "The Edges of Stang," the book went on, "who have been associated with the area for centuries, have often claimed to be descended from this shadowy figure who is supposed to be responsible for so much death and destruction, but other locals have affirmed that this poetic tale has no basis whatever in fact! Indeed, Stang is one of the prettiest villages in this part of Cheshire."

Oliver jotted all this down, then turned to "Cheshire and Its Churches", and found Stang. He discovered that St Elphin was unique to this village church, and that nothing at all was known about him. But there was a fascinating footnote: "It is just possible that St Elphin may be connected with St Elfin's Eve, a moveable feast which always falls on the day before Good Friday. Legend has it that anyone brave enough to sit in the churchyard between twelve and two that night, will see the ghosts of those that are to die within the year, and of those that will suffer misfortune. The end of the procession is always brought up by someone on the point of death." The note ended with two lines from an old Cheshire poem:

*Harmes be to all who over churchyard pass,*
*Grim Death himself shall take the first and last.*

Oliver scribbled furiously. His father had told him quite a lot about Stang, but he was more interested in the salt mining and the old timbered houses. These spooky stories about ghosts and curses were much more interesting, even if they were "a load of old rubbish", in the words of Winnie Webster.

His father hadn't actually given him a project to do this holiday, but Oliver wanted to know more about Stang for his own reasons. There were one or two things he wanted to discuss with Colin and Prill. For a start, he didn't really believe the story about the pile of sandstone blocks collapsing on the dog's foot. His bones told him that Colin had lied about that. There was more to it. But after his remarks in the car they weren't speaking to him. He would have to wait till relations improved a little.

The "office" of the Natural History Society was just a set of dusty filing cabinets in somebody's front room, guarded by an unfriendly turbaned woman who was hoovering the carpet and gloomily dusting stuffed birds in cases. The secretary, her husband—a Mr Bill Stott—was out at work and wouldn't be home till six.

Oliver was polite, but very determined. He made her look at the photograph and watched her closely as she squinted at it through thick glasses. "Mmm . . . a nest, did you say? And you think it's a *what*?"

"A dunnet," said Oliver. "They're quite rare."

"Never heard of it. But as I say, my husband's the bird fanatic. I just dust them, as you see." And she glanced disapprovingly at two moth-eaten owls perched on top of a cabinet. "Now, I've got your name and address. That's all I need. He'll contact you, I expect. I must get on."

Oliver walked slowly down the path as the hoovering started up again. The face was still there, and it was clearer now; the thick, hard mouth was more clearly defined against the branches, the eyes were fiercer, and he thought it was bigger too. That woman hadn't seen it, but

Rose Salt had. For all her odd behaviour he felt closer to Rose than he did to the Blakemans. Perhaps she was like him, rather sensitive to the moods of places, and more aware of what had happened in them centuries ago.

The photograph frightened him. Half of him wanted to tear it into small pieces and throw them in the nearest litter bin. But a voice inside him said, "*No*. That's what They want you to do. Don't you understand anything?" But who were *They*?

He was still looking at the photograph, his fingers sweaty and shaking, when the Stang bus whipped round the corner, turned right, and disappeared into the fog. "*Hey!*" Oliver yelled, dancing about in the road. "This is a request stop. You're supposed to stop here." But all that remained of the bus was a distant rumble of wheels, and the memory of two faces, grinning at him out of the back window.

Oliver started to walk home. If he passed a phone box he'd ring Molly, otherwise he'd thumb a lift. It was absolutely against his mother's rules, but she was miles away, in London, not trudging along an empty road battered by a howling wind and already soaked to the skin as the rain bucketed down from heavy skies.

He eventually turned off the main road at a finger post marked "Stang". This was the way the fire engine must have gone; in this tangle of lanes it had got well and truly lost. At least he could work out where the driver had gone wrong. Who had ever heard of a fire engine not finding a fire? It was incredible, to him.

Several cars swished past, spattering him with mud. Each time he heard an engine he automatically thrust his thumb out. But nobody stopped, or even slowed down. It was as if the skinny little figure in the dripping green anorak was totally invisible.

Then someone screeched to a halt without being asked. "Want a lift, mate?" said a voice. "I'm going down Stang way. That's where you're goin', i'n't it?" Oliver knew who it was without looking. He'd recognised the spanking red motorcycle, the leather trousers and the whiney voice. It was Tony Edge.

He hesitated. He'd never been on a motorcycle, and he wasn't at all sure he could keep his balance. "Er, thanks. But I think I'll walk. It's, er, all fresh air and, well, I'm quite enjoying it." And he stood shivering in the road, looking like a little drowned rat.

Tony Edge gave a loud, unpleasant laugh. "Don't look a gift horse in the mouth, mate. Get on, fer Gawd's sake. You'll be home in five minutes." He leaned down, took Oliver by the arm, and pulled him on to the broad leather seat. "No, *no*. Let me get down," the boy stammered. He didn't like the way the hard fingers gripped his scrawny arms through the great gauntlets, or the hard eyes burning into him with their queer, twisted gleam of triumph, or the awful mouth below the black moustache.

But it was as though the man hadn't heard him. "Hold tight, and keep your knees in," he bellowed above the scream of the engine, and they roared off down a hill, plunging into a thick green mist broken by the tops of bare trees that clutched at them as they tore past, like drowning hands.

It was the longest journey of Oliver's life. Tony Edge careered through the dripping lanes like a thing possessed; fifty, sixty, seventy miles an hour, the great machine bucking and rearing like something in pain, and the dark figure hunched over it, lashing it with streams of foul abuse, screaming curses into the tearing wind, as if the thing were a horse and he was whipping it up to greater and greater speed.

All Oliver could see was a broad, shiny back. As the bike hurtled on, screeching round terrifying bends with a hot smell of rubber, squealing to sudden halts inches away from looming blank walls, he closed his eyes even on that. But the face was in his mind. He could still see those eyes glaring at the road ahead as it leaped and twisted away

67

from him; he could see the awful mouth curve with satisfaction as the wheels sent stones flying in all directions, as birds flew up, and frightened rabbits scuttled for cover.

"Let me get *off*, Tony," Oliver begged. He felt horribly faint and sick, and his head was swimming. "I'm going to fall off," he whimpered ". . . I'm *slipping*." But all the man did was to get up more speed, as they screeched down the hill towards Stang. Then Oliver saw something that might save his life, a man placidly cutting a hedge in the pouring rain, with a green "Ranswick and District" lorry parked in a gateway, and a sign, "STOP, when the light is on red"

Tony rammed his brakes on, and Oliver bided his time, waiting till the cycle was going slowly enough for him to jump off. But something inexplicable was happening. The bike was approaching the red light in slow motion, and Oliver, trying to unstick his trembling fingers from the heavy leather back, found he was slowing down, too, and stopping altogether. His hands slid limply down the black jacket, then froze, stuck to the leather, and he sagged forward, closing his eyes again, not with relief, but because he was unable to move.

A curious tingling was rippling through him now. In a calmer mood he'd have worked out a formula, something involving static electricity, and magnetic forces being drawn towards each other. But all Oliver knew was that he couldn't separate himself from the motorcycle or from Tony Edge, and that if he didn't break free he would die.

He started to cry, and the rider turned round. When the cruel dark eyes met Oliver's a stab of pain surged through him, and a lump stuck in his gullet. It was nothing to do with feeling sick, or the fact that his throat was raw after all his useless pleading. The pain was in the terror, and the terror was in that face.

"Nearly home, mate," a voice said from far away, but not kindly. The innocent remark sounded more like a curse, and the second the light turned green the motorbike surged forward in a final massive explosion of noise and fumes, almost taking off as it breasted the last dark hill, before dropping down into the black valley like a great gout of blood.

"Sorry, kid. Some people can't take speed. Allus makes 'em throw up. Our Sid's the same. See you then. Ta ta." And Tony Edge roared off towards Blake's Pit, leaving Oliver outside Elphins, vomiting into the long grass.

He was there for a long time, heaving and retching, till there was nothing left. His eyes were blurred now, and he had a splitting pain in his head. He stumbled up the garden path and went in at the kitchen door. He was beyond feeling embarrassed about Colin, Prill and the dog, he just wanted to talk to somebody. *Anybody*.

But the kitchen was empty, and only Jessie lay by the smoking fire. When she saw who it was she stopped wagging her tail, put her nose in her paws and closed her eyes again. Oliver looked round helplessly. Where was everyone? Where was Molly? And where was Rose Salt?

He felt abandoned. Slumping down on to a rickety chair he buried his face in his hands, and sobbed.

# Chapter Eight

Prill didn't hear him because she was snooping about in Rose Salt's bedroom, a little attic up some creaky stairs. They'd heard her shuffling about at night when everyone else was in bed. Rose had her own times for doing everything, no one ever seemed to know when she was going out, or when she might be back. Not even Molly.

Wednesday was her day for cleaning the upstairs, and she'd done the children's rooms while they were at the vet's. Prill knew something was different the minute she opened the door, but she couldn't work out what it was at first. Everything was as usual except that it was tidier, and there was a smell of lavender polish. Then she noticed the bed. Her nightdress lay neatly folded on the pillow, but Amy had gone.

She crept up the attic stairs and pushed Rose's door open, startled by the violence of her own emotions. It was only a doll, and Prill was twelve years old, well past the age for teddy bears and pink rabbits. But her mood came from something much deeper. It was part of the cold, barren feeling that was slowly creeping over her face as she stared round Rose's bedroom, remembering all that had happened since they'd come to Stang, and trying to make sense of it.

Horrible pictures crawled through her head, Rose's ghostly figure on the very first night, plucking at the little doll; the bonfire that nobody put out, and that hideous snapping skeleton; the Edge family with their hard, cruel faces, all living near that evil-looking pit. And Jessie? Just what had happened to her? She didn't really believe what Colin had told Molly. It didn't ring true, somehow. Prill knew there was something else, something he hadn't told her.

Rose's room was full of pretty things, every surface was cluttered with ornaments, bottle and pots. On the dressing table there was a basket full of bright hair ribbons. The boys kept cracking jokes about Rose Salt being bald under that pixie-hood. The little collection made Prill sad somehow.

Above the bed was a whole shelf of dolls, all neatly arranged and dusted, some of them quite old. But Amy wasn't among them, so she looked round for the old carpet bag, peeping into the wardrobe and sliding drawers open, even crawling under the bed. But everything was in its place. There was no bag and no doll. The only thing she hadn't investigated was Tony Edge's Slasher costume cut into four purple pieces and laid out on the counterpane. Cautiously Prill felt underneath. No Amy.

She stared out of the tiny window into the sodden field below. The dank meadow, empty of the three horses, had become threatening. She pushed her head out and took deep breaths but the cold air tasted stale, stagnant almost, as if there was no life in it.

Prill sat down on Rose's bed and pulled a crumpled envelope from her pocket. It contained a hilarious letter from Angela Stringer, which had arrived that morning. The riding lessons were obviously not quite what she'd been expecting. "Don't know how you're faring," she wrote, "But I feel like something out of Thelwell. All the ponies are fat and slow, and I always seem to end up with the smallest. My feet usually touch the ground! They're dead strict about what you wear, too. Mum's been going through the church jumble this week, looking for suitable sweaters and things—everyone else looks so *horsey*, my dear, and so well turned out. Gillian and I are definitely the poor relations!

How are you getting on? I think I'll give up this lark, and join the karate course at the Tech. There are some nice boys on that, and I could go with Peter from next door. (Your letter has just arrived! Not before time, please note.) He's not bad, but he obviously doesn't compare with your Tony Edge! Now *he* sounds a thrill a minute . . . Are they really that bad? They can't be. I think you're exaggerating, as usual . . ."

Angela's cheerful prattle brought home, and normality, terribly close. What were they doing here, in this silent, brooding valley, with its tight-lipped, suspicious-looking villagers, its awful sense of waiting, its *secrets*? She pushed the letter back in her pocket, almost wishing it had never come. It had brought too many reminders of ordinariness, of humdrum, day-to-day existence, of the safe, upredictable daily round from which, quite suddenly, they all seemed to have been cut off.

Prill found Colin in the kitchen, with his arm round Oliver. The small boy was still snivelling, and his thin shoulders shook. His lank hair was plastered to his forehead with sweat.

"What on earth's the matter, Oliver?" she said, pulling a stool up on the other side. She forgot about her doll and Rose Salt for a minute, she forgot about Angela's crazy letter. Her cousin was usually so calm and collected, she'd never seen him like this before.

"He says Tony Edge tried to kill him," Colin said, in a small, embarrassed voice. Prill stared at him, wondering if it was some kind of joke, but there was a darkness in his face, and the same blank bewilderment she'd felt herself when she found Amy missing, and the three horses gone from the field.

"Tony Edge *what*?"

"He gave him a lift back from Ranswick on his motorbike. Says he drove like a maniac, and kept going into things. Oll thinks he was trying to throw him off, or something."

"*He was.*"

After all that crying, Oliver's voice was a wavering croak, but the look in his large, pale eyes as he stared up at his cousin was firm enough, and stony with conviction. They'd learned not to quarrel with Oliver when he'd got a bee in his bonnet.

"Well, I can just imagine Tony Edge taking you for a joy ride," Prill said shakily. "He's a rotten driver. Molly said they'd threatened to take his 'L' plates away."

"L for loony," Colin said savagely. "He shouldn't have taken a passenger anyway. It's typical of the Edges."

"Where's Molly?" Prill asked. "Don't you think we should tell her?"

"She's gone to see old Miss Brierley. I don't know where Rose is, but there's something in the oven for lunch, and Molly said we could take that boat out if it stopped raining."

"I don't think I want to," Oliver said, giving a big sniff and rubbing his eyes.

"Oh, come on, Oll," Colin told him. "You said you wanted to practise rowing, and it's a good chance. There's nothing else to do anyway."

"How did you get on at the library?" Prill said, trying to sound casual, but secretly wondering what on earth could have happened between Ranswick and Stang, on the back of that motorbike. "Did you discover anything interesting?"

"Oh, this and that," Oliver replied vaguely. "I copied out bits for my father." Things had improved a little, but not that much. He wasn't ready to say anything yet about Stang and its legends, or to share his suspicions about the Edge family, even though that nightmare ride had made more slot into place.

Prill had decided to keep silent too. It wasn't the right moment to embark upon Rose Salt, and the fact that she was a thief. Colin looked from one to the other, then at Jessie, gloomily nibbling her bandages.

Nobody had pressed him about the accident yet, they'd believed his lies and he'd let them.

After stew, dumplings, and syrup tart, they collected Posie from the Masseys' and walked together as far as Blake's Pit. Only the little girl spoke, prattling away at Prill's side all the way through the village. The three older children were silent and tense, locked in their three separate worlds of suspicion and growing unease.

The old boat belonged to Harold Edge. It was rather decrepit, but actually watertight, and Molly had somehow persuaded him to let the boys borrow it. "Do you think she bribed him?" said Colin, pulling out into the middle of the black, silent water. Oliver stared down as the oars rippled the lake. Water always calmed him, even here, on Blake's Pit. Away from the gloomy trees, and the forlorn-looking cottages, the memory of that terrible journey began to fade a little.

Perhaps he *had* imagined some of it. When you hated people from the start it was hard to see them straight. Tony Edge was probably just a crazy driver who shouldn't be allowed on the road. As they reached the centre of the round pool someone ran out of the caravan and a sharp little voice shouted, "Tek care with that boat!"

"The Puddings are on the warpath," Colin grinned, feeling slightly more cheerful.

Coffin Lane got steeper towards the top of the hill, and Posie grizzled so much that Prill unfolded her blue buggy and strapped her in. She was doing up the buckles when Rose Salt appeared suddenly at her elbow.

"Hello, Posie," she said, and put her hand out, fingering the tight gold curls, admiring the cherry-red anorak and the Fair Isle mittens. The child was perfect, just like a big china doll.

Posie Massey started to cry, and pushed at Rose. "Go 'way," she whimpered. "You '*mell*."

Before Prill could say anything the little brown figure had gone; she watched it making its way back along the rutted track, swinging the old carpet bag, the long mack trailing in the mud, then saw it take the left-hand fork that led to Miss Brierley's cottage.

"That wasn't very nice, Posie," Prill said, pushing the buggy up the stony lane. "That wasn't nice to Rose."

"Don't like Rose," the child said loudly. "Her not nice to Posie."

The track petered out into Stang Heath, a wasteland crossed by the old canal and fenced off into untidy fields. Big Meadow stretched away to the right, disappearing into a dingy fog. Prill stuck her fingers in her mouth, and whistled.

Almost immediately she heard the drumming of hooves. She felt in her pocket for the apples and sugar she'd taken from the kitchen, and within seconds soft noses were pushing at her anorak. Mister and Lucky Lady devoured the apples instantly, with juicy crunching noises, but William, the old carthorse, wasn't there.

Prill gave them the sugar lumps and whistled again, then listened. "William," she hollered, cupping her mouth in her hands. "Willyam. . . *Willum*! Posie Massey cheeped beside her, and as they stood at the gate the mist suddenly thinned out, giving them a clear view of the field. It was empty, apart from the two chestnuts.

A feeble sun was struggling to get through, and Posie wanted to go on. Her father sometimes took her to see the barges, further along the canal. But Prill turned the buggy round smartly, strapped her in again and set off for the village.

Goldilocks whined all the way home. "Sun's shining now," she complained, twisting about and trying to stand up. "Don't *want* to go home. Don't *want* to play with Sam. Sam naughty." But Prill took no notice, she was thinking of William, not spoiled Posie Massey, and when the child tipped the buggy over in her efforts to get out, she lost her

75

temper. "Shut *up*, will you!" she screamed, and gave her an almighty slap.

The little girl's hand flew to her face, and she started to wail. "Posie, Posie," pleaded Prill, kneeling down in the lane. "I'm sorry, darling, but I—"

"Pose *hurt*," the toddler squealed, great tears rolling down her cheeks. "I want Mummy now!" And when she took her hand away, Prill saw a big red mark.

She was appalled at the way she'd lashed out. She'd never hit Alison, never ever; it was against all the rules with someone else's child, and she'd only wanted to go for a walk. Prill found a handkerchief, wet it in a puddle and dabbed Posie's face with it, then she gave her some stale Smarties from the fluff at the bottom of her coat pocket, and the sniffing child settled down to chew them.

She didn't know what had come over her, hitting an innocent little girl, and yelling at her like that. William was only an old horse, she'd never even sat on his back. But she felt more and more uneasy.

Our Vi was opening Winnie Webster's front gate as they went past. She was dolefully practising spellings from a list. "'Receipt. . . Receive . . . "i" before "e" except after "c",'" she muttered.

"Do you know where William is?" Prill called out.

Vi scowled, and lifted her heavy-lidded eyes unwillingly from the book. She didn't like this posh girl from down south, or her brother, or that creep with the glasses that was related to Molly Bover. "William? Who's William when he's at home?" There was nobody in Stang by that name.

"You know. Don't those horses belong to your father?"

The girl stared at her, then light dawned slowly on the pasty face. "Oh, *them*. I dunno. Why ask me?" And she stomped up Winnie's garden path without a backward glance.

Prill left the injured Posie in a hurry, and made a quick getaway before her mother asked any awkward questions. She was rather ashamed of what had happened, but there was no way she could explain her mood to Brenda Massey. Sid Edge was in the road, propping up a fence as usual. She asked him about the horses too; she put the question three times before he bothered to reply, but she was determined to get an answer. At last it emerged that the old horse had been taken into Ranswick, to get new shoes.

An immense relief flooded through her. For a second she felt like hugging the hapless Sid—crumpled baseball cap, runny nose, and all. It sounded quite plausible. Oliver had spotted a forge in Ranswick, "a real old-fashioned one", he'd said, "with an anvil. The man had a leather apron and everything." The Edges couldn't be so bad after all. Prill knew very little about horses but it was obvious to anyone that William must be near the end of his life, he was lame and slow-moving, he shambled while the other two galloped. It must be years since he'd earned his keep at Pit Farm, so someone in the family must be fond of him.

"He'll be back with the others then, tomorrow?" she prodded.

"S'pose so," (sniff). Sid was staring past her, as if there was something fascinating in the middle of the opposite fence. He seemed quite incapable of looking her straight in the eyes just at that moment.

They spent the evening watching a pathetic Western on Molly's T.V., all huddled round the tiny screen, trying to suck some warmth from the smoky fire which Rose had lit in the sepulchral "best room" at the front of the house. She found the film totally gripping, and sat next to Oliver, "ooing" and "ahing" at the least whiff of excitement.

None of the others was thinking about the plot. Oliver had privately concluded that Tony Edge was mentally deranged. He *had* been trying to hurt him on that bike, and possibly trying to kill him. He'd discussed it with Colin, out on Blake's Pit, and his cousin had confided that he thought the Edges might have something to do with the stone that had fallen off the tower. They'd agreed not to tell Prill yet, she was so nervous, and it was no good giving her bad dreams.

But she had them anyway. Every sweating horse on that screen looked like William, every joyous whinny was a cry for help, from him, and when she went to bed she could think of nothing else.

She tossed about in the dark, trying to warm up, and trying to get comfortable on the lumpy mattress, with that noble head forever in her mind. When at last she drifted off to sleep, all her dreams were about William, but in happier days. The big, tatty ears were smooth and alert, the coat gleamed glossily, and the decrepit old horse was young and strong again, pulling a painted wagon with children aboard in their Sunday best, all laughing and shouting.

But the huge eyes were always turned upon Prill. Wherever William went, trudging along the summer lanes with his chattering load, his face was fixed upon hers, mute, pleading, unutterably sad.

# Chapter Nine

She got up very early next morning, before it was fully light. The low room was stuffy and she'd slept with the window open, in spite of the cold. A smell was drifting up from the field below, something she couldn't identify. Perhaps that had woken her.

She sniffed, and thought, then sniffed again. It was a hot, fishy smell, a bit like strong glue. She put her head out of the window and peered down into the field, then left, towards the village green. Nobody was about yet, and nothing was stirring. It had rained heavily in the night and the trees dripped mournfully into the sopping grass. There were no dogs barking, no bleating of lambs, no birdsong. Prill could never remember such a silent spring.

She slipped on her clothes and stole downstairs. The house was still quiet, but there was a faint snoring from the boys' room. She wondered whether to wake Colin, and ask him to come with her, but he was at his worst when shaken out of a deep sleep. He might snap her head off.

There were certainly signs of life in the Edges' shop. The shabby blue blinds were down, but there was a light behind them, and as she hovered in the road she could hear a faint babble of voices. The fishy smell was much stronger here, and as she tiptoed past she saw Tony Edge's motorbike propped against a nearby wall.

Behind the shop there was an assortment of broken-down sheds. There was a light in one of them, and the voices were drifting out of it. So was the smell. She could see a muddy path leading round the back from the road, ending in an untidy heap of squashed cartons and a rusty butcher's bike with one wheel.

Prill knew, even before she peeped through a knothole in the warped door. The Edges were in there, all huddled round a great boiler. Steam was billowing out of it in thick yellow clouds, and the glue smell was unbearable, but they were all laughing, and clinking glasses, and poking about in the pot with long sticks.

The shed was spiked with hooks with sausages dangling from them. Frank Edge, his back to the drinking party, was gloomily slamming handfuls of chopped meat into a huge mincer and turning a creaky handle. On another hook, higher up, hung something very beautiful, a long switch of creamy white with a dark brown stripe down the middle. At the top it was all bloody and mangled. It was William's tail.

Prill's stomach heaved, and she brought the back of her hand up to her mouth to suppress a scream. But she couldn't get away from the door. Through the knothole, on the far side of the boiler, Tony Edge's eyes seemed riveted on her, like some awful magician willing her to see his trick through to the bitter end.

Suddenly, a tap was opened at the bottom of the pot, near the floor, and a sticky brown broth poured out over the tiles, disappearing down a drain in the middle. Then Tony reached down inside, his face disappearing in clouds of steam. Harold did the same, and together they pulled out their dripping trophy and held it up for everyone to see.

"It's not boiled enough," someone yelled. "It can't be. It'll tek us ages that will, Tone."

"Oh, get scrapin and shut up," Prill heard, and there was the sound of knives and cleavers being chucked on to the floor, and people fighting to get them.

She forced her eyelids apart and looked first at Tony, then at the steaming head. It was still William's face, though the eye sockets were now black and empty, and Tony's hands had disappeared up inside where the neck had been severed from the body.

Prill's eyes filled with tears. The youth dropped his gaze at last, and she stumbled blindly away down the slimy path. They had wanted her to come. They had wanted her to see what they had made, out of that trusting, innocent creature. It was as if they'd uttered a spell over their bubbling pot. "Bring Prill," they'd chanted, as she slept on at Elphins. "Get Prill Blakeman to come. She'd like this."

Molly was standing at her front door in an old red dressing gown, peering out anxiously into the wet morning. "*Prill*," she said, catching her breath. "What on earth . . ." But Prill had slumped against her. "Molly," she wept. "They've got William. He hadn't gone for new shoes at all. They're . . . *wicked*, Molly. They were really enjoying it . . ."

The bewildered woman wrapped her arms round Prill and guided her down the passage into the warm kitchen. She said nothing till they both had mugs of tea, Prill's with three spoonfuls of sugar in it. Then she looked at the bewildered, tear-stained face with anxious eyes.

"Did you *know*, Molly?" the girl suddenly shrieked accusingly. "Did you *know* they were going to do that? You knew, didn't you? Molly, why didn't you stop them?"

Molly Bover never told lies. "Prill, dear," she began slowly. "Of course I didn't know. But you see . . . well, the Edge family . . . you don't need to tell me what they're like, do you? Poor George *did* throw their horse on the bonfire, and old William *was* theirs, you know, to do what they liked with. He was ready for the knacker's yard, dear. Ask anyone."

"Yes, but to do *that*," Prill sobbed. "They'd obviously been there all *night* . . . it was a kind of party in there, they were all drinking. Why do things like that at *night*, if you're not ashamed of them?"

"I'm not defending them, Prill," Molly said quietly, "I've lived in this village for nearly fifty years, and I know what they're like. Winnie tried to get them to borrow the

81

Saltersly head, but they wouldn't have it. They said it would bring bad luck or something. Oh, I don't know . . ." she finished lamely.

"You see, dear," she tried again, taking Prill's cold hand in her own. "Real country people can't afford to be too sentimental. Now I *know* it's grisly, and one of their more awful customs, but it does go right back. It isn't the first horse's head to be boiled down behind that shop, dear, and I wish you'd not seen it. But think of that calf Jimmy Bostock delivered the other day. Awful things happen, you know, and when you live with them, day in day out, you get a bit hard."

"What calf?" Prill said.

Molly Bover could have kicked herself. She opened her mouth, then shut it again abruptly, and felt in her pocket for a bottle of pills. "Now look, Prill, I'm giving you half of one of these. I'm having one too. It's only half-past five and we need a bit more sleep. When we get up we can have a nice leisurely breakfast. Nothing much on today, thank goodness. And we'll fix up your riding lessons, first thing."

There was a silence. Molly obviously wasn't going to tell her about the calf. "All right," she said blankly. Anything to get out of Stang. She wanted nothing more to do with this village and its barbaric play. She wouldn't help with the costumes, watch rehearsals, or *anything*.


Oliver had been listening on the other side of the door. As Prill went up the stairs, he slid out of the shadows and into the kitchen. "What calf?" he said, pulling up a stool and inspecting the contents of the teapot. "What was wrong with it?"

"Oliver," Molly said wearily. "I was just going back to bed. Have a cup of tea by all means, but I'm off."

"What calf though?"

"Well, it arrived a couple of days ago, one of Jack Edge's. It was . . . rather deformed."

"How?"

She took a deep breath. Prill had been calmed down with sweet tea and half a sleeping pill, for the moment anyway. But this cousin of hers, with his penetrating little voice, and cold, all-seeing stare, was a more complicated kettle of fish. She couldn't pull the wool over his eyes.

"Well, if you must know, Oliver, the poor thing had two heads—well, the beginnings of a second. They had to kill it. Dreadful really, but it does happen, more often with lambs though. There's something like this every spring."

She expected Oliver to lose his colour, if not faint, but he looked perfectly calm as he stirred his tea. "Anne Boleyn had six fingers on one hand," he said thoughtfully. "My father told me that. And . . . and some babies are born with hair all over their faces. That's the same thing really."

"Yes, Oliver," Molly said helplessly, tightening the cord of her dressing gown. "Yes, I suppose it is." She went up to bed feeling completely at a loss. This infuriating child really was a gold mine of useless information.

# Chapter Ten

Prill didn't go riding that day. Molly was picking up the phone to ring the stables when Brenda Massey flung the kitchen door open. "Have you seen Posie?" she burst out. She'd been crying; her eyes were puffy and her frizzy blonde hair was in a wild tangle round her face.

"No," Molly said, peering about, as if the child might be hiding somewhere. "We were up rather late, I'm afraid. We've only just finished breakfast."

"She was in the playroom; we got up at six today, George had to go to Newcastle, he's filming. She had her breakfast with us, then refused to go back to bed. Sam needed feeding so I went upstairs again, and I nodded off in the chair. When I came down again, she'd gone. *She's just not there, Molly.*"

"Sit down a minute. Now where's Sam?"

"At home, with Mrs Cotton. She comes in to clean on Thursdays. He's all right, he's asleep anyway. Molly, where *is* she?"

"Have you phoned George?"

"No."

"Good. Don't. She'll turn up in a few minutes."

"Molly, I've *looked*."

"Listen, dear, the three children are getting dressed, they're sensible. I'll send them round the village. Let's be systematic. There's no point in having alarums and excursions when she's probably shut in somewhere, or playing in someone's house. You've looked in all the cupboards and things at home, have you?"

"Well, of course I have," Brenda shrieked, and the tears rolled down her face.

"Sorry. Silly question. Now was she still in her pyjamas?"

"No, she got dressed when George did. And—and her anorak's missing, *and* the buggy. She likes pushing it round the village."

"Well then, I expect that's what she's doing, dear. What colour's this anorak?"

"Red."

"Marvellous. That's easily spotted, anyway. Now you go back to Sam, and I'll get the kids organized."

"Will your Rose help?" sniffed Brenda, dabbing her eyes. Molly Bover always made her feel better, she was so big, and cheerful, and calm. Her panic subsided a little as she got up from the table.

"I expect so," Molly said vaguely, but she didn't call her into the kitchen. Rose Salt was missing. She'd not done the breakfast, or taken the dogs out. Jessie was lying peacefully by the fire with the two other poodles nuzzling up to her like young piglets. They all looked quite happy together, for once.

Molly slung her tattered cape round her shoulders rather irritably. Rose would choose this moment to go off on one of her secret little jaunts; she didn't do it very often these days. Why pick this morning? She'd give her a good talking to when she came in, though heaven only knew when that might be.


After three hours the police were called in. Everyone in the village turned out to hunt for Posie Massey, old wardrobes were emptied, sheds unlocked and searched, allotments combed. There was a terrible moment when someone prised open an old fridge on the local dump. But there was no sign inside of the little red anorak, or the buggy, just a vile smell.

George was making a T.V. film in Newcastle. The team were on location, shooting at a castle somewhere up the coast. By midday they still hadn't contacted him. "They'll get hold of him, dear," Molly said placidly, patting Brenda's hand. They were in the Masseys' kitchen, drinking yet another cup of tea. "In a way it might be better if they don't. She'll turn up soon, and he'll come home wondering what all the fuss was about."

But she was worried now. Rose Salt still hadn't come back, and Molly had been forced to tell the police she was missing. The young officer who jotted the details down didn't seem very interested; he had dozens of addresses to check, and besides, he knew all about Rose. He'd been brought up in the next village. There was no rhyme or reason to what that daft girl did, but she wasn't up to kidnapping a child and going into hiding.

Colin, Oliver and Prill ended up on an old bench outside the village pub, looking dumbly at the squad of police cars. They were tired out after wandering all over Stang Heath with Molly, going to various friends and neighbours, and meeting with the same unhelpful stares.

"What do you think can have happened, Oll?" Colin muttered. He didn't dare ask Prill. She was sitting white-faced and silent, thinking about her little sister. Alison could have been in that fridge, or face down in one of the salt pits, or a greenish, swollen lump drifting gently down the old canal. There was so much water round Stang. They were talking of bringing frogmen in, if the child wasn't found.

Oliver had been trotting after Molly with his notebook. Before answering Colin's question he checked down a list carefully. "Well, they're looking in Big Meadow at the moment," he said very precisely. "They've got six officers up there, going over every inch of ground. If she's not there—her body, I mean—I should think they'd start dragging."

Colin wished he'd not asked. Oliver had this uncanny knack of spelling out everyone's worst fears. And he could be so unfeeling. He pronounced the "body" as if it was a sack of potatoes. Prill suddenly got up from the bench and walked away. "I'm going back to Elphins," she said grimly. "It's pointless, just sitting here."

The Edges had got to know that Rose Salt was missing, and Jack came up to tackle Molly about it. Through the closed kitchen door the children listened to a violent argument. "Find Rose Salt," he was bellowing, "and you'll find the child. She's a nutcase, I've always said so." Then they heard Molly. "There's the door, Jack. Go through it, will you. The police know all about Rose, I told them myself." Her voice was quite savage, and she slammed the door so hard it shook the house. She wasn't always sweet and kind.

The family had come out in force to help in the search, but they were no real use to anyone. The officer in charge of the dump told Sid and Violet to clear off in the end. They seemed to find the grisly hunt for clues rather entertaining, and Sid kept digging up "treasures" on the smelly rubbish heaps. "Look a' this, Vi," and part of an old pram was chucked over, then some piping. "Copper, that is. We could take it to the rag man in Ranswick."

Wherever the Edges gathered there was knowing talk of Rose Salt. "Find Rose Salt and you'll find the child," rang in Colin's ears as he watched Sid's father storm down the village street. They were like parrots, all of them, pecking over the coming disaster, and looking forward to a juicy discovery later in the day.

George Massey got home as the last light drained out of the valley, and the flashing police lights splashed the old cottages with eerie blue shadows. It was too dark to search any more, but the hunt would start again at dawn, and more men would be brought in. He spent his evening sitting by the silent telephone, his face like ash, not even bothering to take his coat off. Brenda was asleep ustairs, drugged to death with tranquilizers, and old Mrs Cotton was trying to keep Sam quiet. He bawled so hard she thought the Edges might come round from their shop, and complain.

At eight o'clock Molly remembered that nobody had been up with Miss Brierley's supper. "Don't go out, Molly," Prill pleaded. She didn't want to be left in that cold, dark house on her own, with Rose missing, and Posie Massey not found, and Jessie now whining miserably over her sore leg, and snapping at the other dogs.

"We'll go," Colin said, slipping his coat on and picking up the little casserole of stew. "Come on, Oll, we might hear something. Noises travel further at night. When they saw anoraks being pulled on, the poodles got excited and began leaping up and barking. "No," Colin said firmly. "We're not taking you two, not tonight."

"Certainly not," said Oliver, eying the silly creatures with great distaste. Why did people have dogs? "Go back to your substitute mother," he advised coldly.

The walk through Stang was rather unnerving; Molly had given them a big torch, but the darkness was thick and pressed on them as they hurried along, swallowing up the path behind. As they climbed up towards Blake's End, Colin shone the beam back on the waters of the pit, half hoping they might see something, dreading what it might be. But the sullen water was like black glass, secret and undisturbed, reflecting a moonless night.

Old Miss Brierley was sitting up and quite perky. There was a fire in the grate, and a smell of frying. She asked them to put the casserole in the scullery, for tomorrow, because she'd had a good supper already. Colin wondered if Rose Salt had been in. The cottage was swept and tidy, and the old woman knew all about the missing child.

She liked these nice boys from Molly's, and she was all set to chat. But listening was difficult, the room was so airless and stuffy, and Oliver didn't like the sound of her breathing. She was going downhill now. His friend Mr Catchpole had been like this, at the end. Colin obviously didn't realise how ill the old woman was, but then he didn't understand about elderly people.

She set off at a gallop but tired amost at once. She mentioned the Edge family, and they pricked their ears up. She was ninety years old so she must have a lot of interesting stories to tell. But she was soon drifting. The effort of talking was clearly too much and she lay back on the pillows, and closed her eyes. It was as if all the words in the world were floating past, like leaves on a river, and she had to pluck them out, one by one. "Water," she whispered. "When the waters drop, and the city rises, that means evil."

Colin looked at his cousin. "She means Blake's Pit," Oliver said quietly. "Don't interrupt her."

"Bad luck," she murmured. "Only been seen twice in my lifetime . . . Once the day before war broke out, and before that . . . Oh, I forget, duckie."

"*When?*" prompted Oliver. But the sharp question was too loud. She jumped, a coal fell down in the fire, and Colin clutched his arm. "You're frightening her, Oll. Leave her alone. She's wandering. It can't be that important."

But Oliver knew that it was. He waited tensely in the silence, willing the old woman not to fall asleep. Then, after a few minutes of jumbled muttering, she half sat up in bed and said quite clearly, "April Fourteenth, that's when it was."

"That was last Friday," Colin said dumbly. But she repeated distinctly, "April Fourteenth, 1912," then "I'm going to sleep now, dearies. Thank Molly for that nice stew."

On the walk back to Elphins the boys didn't speak to each other. The heavy silence wrapped itself round them, unbroken by the smallest noise. There were no dogs barking, no lost child screaming in a dark and lonely place, only their own thoughts, wriggling about in their aching brains like little angry snakes.

Oliver was thinking about his notebook. Perhaps he should go back to the library and see if he could find out more about Blake's Pit. He was more and more convinced that the Edges were the real clue to all that was happening. If only people didn't get old and worn-out,

Miss Brierley might be able to help him. But she was dying. "April 14th 1912"—what did it mean? Oliver was good on dates, but he didn't associate that one with anything.

Then he remembered another April day. He'd gone up to Stang churchyard that morning, and watched two police officers poking about in the long grass. "Eliza, Jane and Thomas Massey, infants, tragically lost on the night of 21st April 1853." According to the church guidebook they were the children of a wealthy farmer, and they'd been mysteriously drowned in Blake's Pit. Their bodies hadn't been found till months afterwards. "21st April"—the date on the mouldering gravestone burned in his memory. It was tomorrow.

# Chapter Eleven

Before they got up next day the police had been and gone again. A squad car was parked by the Green, with an officer inside, talking into a radio, but the search had been shifted to the other villages, and they were dragging the canal. The Masseys' house was shut up and silent, with the curtains pulled across, as if someone had died. A young policeman stood by the front door, but nobody was allowed in.

Molly insisted on taking Prill to the stables, and Oliver went with them, for the car ride. He wanted to quiz her about the Edges, though he'd decided she didn't like him very much and might not tell him anything. Still, he could try. It was better than taking those awful dogs out again.

Colin walked them up to Winnie Webster's. She'd know what had happened on April 14th 1912, her general knowledge was fantastic, according to Molly. The village kids called her Brain of Britain. He found her in her greenhouse, potting seedlings. "Sinking of the Titanic," she said, the minute she heard his question. "Why do you . . . ah, I know. You've been talking to Kath Brierley, haven't you?"

Colin's mouth fell open. How could Winnie know that? Did people in Stang have a second sight or something? Did this village drive everybody a bit crazy? "Yes, yes I have," he stammered. "But how do you know?"

"*Well*," she said crisply, shaking soil off her gardening gloves. "It was on the Titanic that—no, go inside and look for yourself. I'll have finished this in a jiffy. Big bookcase, bottom shelf, Volume Twelve of the blue encyclopaedia. *Don't bend it back*."

The book gave a passenger list of all the people who'd

drowned when the "unsinkable" ship, Titanic, on its maiden voyage to America, struck an iceberg and sank on the night of April 14th 1912. Among them Colin found a Percy Brierley, described as a Manchester cotton millionaire. "He was an uncle," Winnie explained, peering over his shoulder. Kath's was a poor branch of the family, just tenant farmers, here in Stang. And I suppose she told you how she and her brother Wilf were out on Blake's Pit that night, larking about in a boat? And how they saw Old Stang, down in the water? And I suppose she told you that she saw it again, in 1939, the day before war was declared?"

"Well, she hinted," Colin said uncertainly.

*"By glimmer of scale and gleam of fin,*
*Folks have seen them all."*

Molly's deep, musical voice came back to him in the cluttered room, making Winnie's snappy remarks sound like the cawing of rooks.

"She's a very old lady, dear, don't forget that. And she's upset about this Massey business. Aren't we all? Memory plays funny tricks, you know, and people make things fit, to match their theories. Kath Brierley's always romanced, and I don't think there's a shred of truth in what she says. I don't believe in luck, good or bad. What comes to us in life we bring upon ourselves, dear, through our own efforts. Now then, it's coffee time. Would you like a cup?"

Winnie Webster was hard, for all her good deeds. Posie Massey was missing, presumed drowned, old Miss Brierley was near her end, and all she could talk about was "making an effort". It was as much as the poor woman could do to raise her head.

"No, thank you," he said bleakly, and after a few minutes he got up and went home.

At about three that afternoon the children were coming down the hill from Blake's End when they saw a small procession making its way along Coffin Lane. They thought Posie had been found at first; four men in shiny black suits were walking slowly towards the pit, carrying something yellow between them. Prill froze, then she realized that the stretcher blankets were red, not yellow, and it was much too big to be a little child. When they reached the water's edge she saw that it was a rubber dinghy. The whisper went round the village like wildfire. They'd found nothing in the canal yet. Blake's Pit was next.

Colin wondered if they ought to go back to Elphins, it was ghoulish just hanging around, but Oliver had already marched up to the frogmen and stood with some other boys, watching them unpack their equipment. Prill stood all alone, by a great willow tree, her hands dangling limply at her sides, staring out across the sullen water, her face tearless and blank.

The frogmen struggled into flippers, adjusted heavy harnesses and checked oxygen cylinders. People wandered down from the village in silent little groups and stood watching, at a distance. But the Edges weren't there. Colin wouldn't have put it past Harold and Frank to shut their shop up, in case they missed something, but he couldn't see them in the crowd. Sid and Tony weren't there either, and the door of the rusty caravan remained firmly shut.

It was Colin who first noticed Rose Salt. She was making her way down one of the little tracks that led from the Heath to join the path that went round Blake's Pit, and she was pushing something. When she saw the crowd she waved, and Colin waved back, but at the same moment one of the frogmen signalled to the bank, and the babble of voices on the police radios changed to a high, monotonous bleep.

A stillness fell upon the watchers. The police officers exchanged looks and walked quickly from their cars to the water's edge. "Hello," Rose shouted cheerfully, not really understanding why nobody was taking any notice of her. "Hello, everyone, look what I found on the Heath." And she started to pick her way down towards the muddy path, pushing Posie's blue buggy with the old shopping bag strapped into the seat, like a sleeping child.

As if from nowhere, from the very hedges and ditches, figures appeared and began to move slowly towards her. The caravan door was open now, and a string of small figures trooped out of it, creeping towards Rose. The crowd at the pit had suddenly thickened. They saw Tony Edge, and Sid too, sidling away from the others and making their way up the hill. "Let's ask her what she's got in that damned bag," someone said. "Don't believe she *found* that pushchair. Do you?"

Rose was soon surrounded and Colin looked across anxiously at the police and the frogmen, expecting them to row rapidly to shore, to intervene and get the poor girl out of trouble. But he saw, to his horror that they were busy pulling a dripping bundle out of the water and into the boat; they had no eyes for what was happening behind them, on the slimy green slope. All the Edges seemed to be there now, in a solid ring round the terrified Rose, hurling questions at her.

"What you bin up to, Rose Salt?" Sid yelled. "Police bin lookin' for you."

"Give over," Jack Edge told him savagely. "Get back to the others, will you? Now listen, Rose," he began. "A child's gone missing. You know that, don't you?"

"Where d'you get that pushchair?" one of the Puddings squealed, like a stuck pig. "They've bin on the lookout for that pushchair."

Rose Salt looked in terror from one to the other. She was confused and the strange questions frightened her. "I went to me auntie's in Brereton Cross," she whimpered. "She's got bad legs. The house needed bottoming."

"But what about that pushchair?" Tony Edge bellowed.

"I found it up there, under them trees, thought I'd just—" But fear swallowed her speech. The Edges were terribly close to her now, their dark bristly faces were thrust right up against her, like huge rats, and the older children had sticks in their hands.

From the water's edge the crowd watched the pathetic little figure slithering downhill, the pixie-hood bobbing idiotically, the brown mack flapping. "Come off it, Rose," someone shouted. "Where's the kid? You've bin hiding her, haven't you? Think there's a reward out or summat?" And with great crowing noises the Edges pursued her down the slimy grass, laughing to each other, and pointing, and waving their sticks.

Rose couldn't stop now, she was going too fast. The flimsy buggy, weighed down by the heavy bag, pulled her along. Heavy rain during the morning had turned the main track into a river of mud and slippery stones. Rose shot across it without even stopping and began to career down the few remaining feet, faster and faster as the bank dropped away to nothing, towards the glinting black water. There was no real shore on that side of the valley.

Suddenly, both feet flew out from under her, she lost a shoe in the mud, and with a great scream she half slid, half fell into the pit, thrashing about and making hideous quacking noises which were abruptly cut off as the icy waters met over her head. There was no bank, no tree or bush to cling on to, nothing to save her. The buggy, with the contents of the bulging bag now dropping out of it, hit the water with a great wallop, and floated about for a while till it got caught up in a mass of drifting tree branches. But everyone had their eyes fixed on Rose as she plunged about in terror, making awful gobbling sounds as she tried to keep afloat, the baggy old mack filling with air like a brown balloon.

She couldn't swim but she wasn't going to drown without a struggle. The Edges stood above the lake in a black knot, watching the helpless, screaming figure, and saw two of the frogmen swim over to her, each taking an arm and flipping her over on to her back. Within seconds she was in the boat, and Colin saw them chuck the sodden lump of rags overboard again. His knees almost buckled under him with sheer relief. So it couldn't be Posie, and there was still a chance that the child was still alive.

Rose Salt certainly was, and a few minutes later they were all on the other side. The frogmen were swaddling her in blankets, and the policemen were bending over her, and she was screaming the same sentence over and over again. "Bin to me auntie's at Brereton Cross. Bad legs. House needed bottoming."

"All right, Rose," they kept saying. "It's all right now. Let's just get you home." But she was making such a racket that nobody noticed the tiny figure at the top of Coffin Lane, a miniature silhouette against the lead-coloured sky. Only when Rose paused for breath did they hear the baby cry of greeting, like the cheep of a bird. "Hello, Prill," it called out. "I'm hungry now. Go home to Sam and Mummy now. I'm *cold*."

There were no signs at all that Posie Massey had been wandering over Stang Heath for twenty-four hours. She was immaculate. The blue dungarees and cherry-red anorak were spotless, so were the shoes and the little white socks. Her face was shiningly clean, and the gold curls clustered round her head like a halo.

When the policeman took her in his arms and walked briskly up the hill towards the village she didn't cry or protest, she simply announced that she wanted her mother, and a drink of juice. She couldn't say where she'd been. All she ever said, when they asked, was "Dark . . . dark . . ." and if they persisted she started to cry.

# Chapter Twelve

It was awful at Elphins that night. Molly shoved them all into the damp sitting room, with plates of bread and cheese, and said they could watch television for the evening. Nobody wanted to, and nobody felt very hungry. With no Rose around to coax the fire into life, it remained a feeble dribble in the grate. They sat hunched over it miserably, empty and shivering, chewing on the cold food and thinking of her gorgeous soups and stews. "Molly just can't be bothered with us," Prill grumbled. "I wish we could go home. I hate it here."

"Don't be so daft," Colin exploded. "That's just selfish. How do you think she feels, with policemen crawling all over the house?"

"Only two." But Prill felt uncomfortable, all the same. It was dreadful for Molly, and when she'd seen them carrying Rose up the garden path she'd looked an old, old woman, trembling and grey-faced.

"But where on earth did Rose *go* with her? That's what I'd like to know," Colin said. "The kid looked so clean and everything, as if she'd been through a car wash."

"Well, they must have got it out of her by now," Prill mumbled, through a mouthful of bread. "They've been questioning her for hours, and she'd made enough noise about it."

Oliver gave a queer little smile and jabbed at the fire with a poker. "What are you grinning at?" Colin demanded rather irritably. "Do you think it's funny or something?"

His cousin said nothing. "Funny" was the last thing he thought; he smiled because he believed he knew the truth about Posie Massey's disappearance, and because it was awful and beyond anyone's understanding. It was that nervous, idiotic smile that sometimes creeps across the face when a person gets terrible news, when words don't mean anything any more, and tears aren't enough.

"I expect Molly will tell us tomorrow," he said calmly, putting down the poker and standing up. "I'm going to bed, it'll be warmer. Is anyone else coming? Molly's put the bottles in."

She had asked them not to go into the kitchen, but as they went up the stairs they could hear Rose Salt loud and clear, still protesting to the police that she'd found the buggy on Stang Heath, and about Aunt Elsie's bad legs.

Molly didn't go to bed till one in the morning. When the police had gone, and she managed to get Rose to sleep, she wandered into her studio with the dogs padding after her, wondering whether to start packing the kiln. She'd planned to do a firing this week. But arranging the pots on their various shelves was painstaking, laborious work. She was tired out and her hands wouldn't stop shaking. She decided to leave it till tomorrow, she'd feel calmer then.

On her way to her room she peeped in on the three children. The old oil lamp she carried round at night cast its soft light on their sleeping faces. They all looked so peaceful, Oliver neatly tucked up like a parcel, Colin with parted lips and one hand under his head, the girl quite still, her thick auburn hair tumbling over the pillow.

But they didn't make Molly feel peaceful. Nothing had gone right since these three had arrived in Stang. She looked at them again; Oliver worried her somehow, he was so adult in the way he looked at everything, and he asked such penetrating questions. In ghost stories it was children like that who made things "happen".

And yet she didn't believe in ghosts, or in "luck", any more than Winnie Webster did. What was she going to tell them about the child's disappearance? She didn't understand it herself, and neither did the police. It seemed that Rose Salt's story was perfectly true, they'd been over to check. Aunt Elsie's little house had been as clean as a new pin, and the old woman sitting cheerfully by a good fire, saying she hoped Rose wouldn't leave it so long next time. Just what had happened to little Posie Massey was still a complete mystery, and the police were baffled in spite of all their efforts.

Molly fell asleep the minute her head touched the pillow. Colin slept too, wrestling with the frogmen in Blake's Pit. Prill's dreams were of horses, thousands of them, rising up from huge cauldrons and staring at her with that pitiless Edge face.

Only Oliver didn't dream. He knew the police file on Posie Massey would be closed eventually, and that no tramp or lunatic would ever be turned in for questioning. There were simply no procedures to deal with what had happened, but nobody understood that yet except him. He knew also that in spite of that witch-hunt this afternoon, the Edges weren't to blame either.

Something had been unleashed in Stang, something to do with that family and the black lake they lived by. It had forced him on to that nightmare ride with Tony Edge, it had nearly killed Jessie; today it had turned time on its head and spirited away a little child. In Stang churchyard three Massey children lay dead and rotten, "tragically lost" in Blake's Pit one hundred and thirty years ago to the day. It just couldn't be coincidence.

Why was all this happening? Why now? It was as if a dragon, thousands of years asleep, had woken up ravenous and roamed the land. He wondered what was going to happen next in this village, and what anyone could do to stop it. *What could he do*?

It was typical of Oliver to fall asleep before actually deciding. Two things were obvious, the Massey child was safe and well, and Rose Salt was not to blame.

There might be rather a lot to do in the morning and a good night's rest was the best preparation for whatever lay ahead.

When it was all over they said he must have dreamt it all, but Colin knew it had happened. Oliver's snoring had woken him up, and that was real enough. When he turned over on his back his mouth dropped open and he made an irritating snuffling noise, quiet enough, but rhythmic and monotonous, just the thing to drive you bananas in the middle of the night.

He thought about his cousin as he walked through Stang. "I couldn't stop myself," Oliver had blurted out in Molly's kitchen, after that weird episode on Tony Edge's motorbike. "I didn't *want* to go with him. I wanted to walk. He *made* me." And it was all Colin could ever say about what happened that night.

He'd opened his eyes to hear the church clock striking three, and felt wide awake at once. His mind was in tumult, filled with a jumble of faces, the Edge tribe turned into horses, rats, and poodles, a crowing rabble that forced Rose into a pit of darkness, filling her mouth with mud. And in his nightmare there was an undertow of the most terrible crying, mothers weeping for their children, a sound so desolate and bleak it seemed to embrace the sadness of the whole world.

He didn't want to be walking through Stang at three in the morning. Why couldn't he be tucked up in bed like the others? But something had lured him out of Elphins, like an animal towards a snare, and he found himself walking through the sleeping village in bright moonlight, towards the waiting waters of Blake's Pit.

He didn't dare lift his face till he was clear of the cottages, but concentrated on his feet, clambering up the rutted track that led away from the shore, up towards the Edges' farm. Whatever drew him now was so powerful, so hard to resist, that Colin dreaded looking up in case he saw someone standing there, some dark and terrible shape with its finger beckoning, Harold or Frank, the big bullying Jack, even Sid or Our Vi. It didn't matter who it was. They were all one.

But the gloomy farmhouse was dark and silent, and there was no figure lowering over him. He stopped and looked back at the silent, moonlit valley, and saw for the first time that there was a direct line between Pit Farm and St Elphins, with its strange, lopsided steeple. There were no trees or houses in the way, and the ugly line of telegraph poles marched away to his left, across fields. From here the Edges must have always looked across on Stang, on its huddle of cottages, its pub and its church, on all its living and all its dead.

"God's finger pointing up to heaven"—that's what Grandma Blakeman had always told him about church steeples, in her bedtime stories, years ago, when he was little. But Stang spire was crooked and deformed. It was almost as if it cringed away from the brooding farmhouse, and its devilish crew; it was as if, centuries ago, one of them had put the evil eye on it and knocked it sideways . . . Colin knew that was ridiculous; he understood all about the leaning buildings in Cheshire, and the salt pits, and the subsidence, perfectly well.

Even so, a stab of cold made him shiver violently, but it was nothing to do with the chilly night, or the clear brilliance of the moon and stars. It was a cold that sliced through him like shock waves, turning his legs to jelly, prickling his flesh. He'd felt it the first time he'd seen Tony Edge, and when Rose had fallen into the pit. Oliver must have felt it too, as he careered along the lanes on that lunatic ride.

Was that story about the beggar just a legend? Molly had told them Blake's Pit was cursed. Did it matter that it all happened centuries ago? Did it make the evil less? In the last few days they'd seen enough horror in this village to last them a lifetime. "That family can't seem to help

101

itself, somehow." Molly had said that, at the beginning. One of their ancestors must have cursed the old city into the lake, but had somehow cursed himself also, and all who came after. The Edges were tainted.

Weak legs carried him down to the pit. He settled himself in the dinghy and took up the oars. Like a man in a dream, not asking why, he rowed out strongly into the middle of the lake, rippling the still water like black silk. All he cared about now was distancing himself from the looming mass of Pit Farm; he was breaking the scent, like a hunted animal that crosses a stream.

When he reached the middle he rested on his oars, listening to the night sounds. A dog barked somewhere, and a light went on in a cottage. He thought of Prill and Oliver, tucked up in bed at Elphins, and of old Miss Brierley dying at Blake's End; he wondered whether Posie was asleep, curled up with her mother for safety.

There was a lot of debris bobbing about on top of the water, bits of old rag and what looked like lumps of soggy newspaper. He peered over the side, thinking about Rose's bulging bag. It was still in the lake presumably. One drifting mass was much bigger than the rest and for one horrible moment Colin thought he was clutching at the shoulders of a floating corpse. But it was only a wadge of sodden rags, caught up with some drifting tree branches. He pulled it on board, and dropped it into the bottom of the boat.

Then he stared over the side for a second time, suddenly aware that it was getting lighter. But the sun didn't rise at three in the morning, not even in Stang, and as he looked down into the water he realized that the strange brightness was coming from below.

The murderous black pit had become as clear as glass, and he saw a whole city, white, beautiful, as if frosted over by the first snow of winter. He saw little cottages and great manor houses, he saw rows of tiny shops, he saw a church and a castle, with pinnacles and domes, and flags flying

102

from spiked turrets. But he saw no people there, no sign that man had ever been, only the creatures of the lake, drifting in and out of windows and doors on their silent ways.

All his life Colin would remember it, being alone on the round, black lake, staring down at the forgotten city, wondering how it had been for them. Was it like Pompeii? Had the waters come upon them like that burning lava flow, sweeping over old men in doorways, over women chatting in the streets? And were the faces of the children eaten away by fish?

The vision faded, the water thickening and turning dead and cold.

*"In a king's tower and a queen's bower,*
*The fishes come and go . . ."*

As he rowed back, Molly's voice rang in his head like a bell, and mingled with the croak of old Kath Brierley. "Evil," she'd told them. "When the city rises it means evil." And now he, Colin Blakeman, had seen the drowned city for himself. What did it mean?

Within minutes he was back on dry land, and hitching the boat to its rusty ring with shaking fingers. He wanted reality now, a fresh hot-water bottle and a mug of cocoa, Oliver snorkling away in the next bed. What on earth was he doing out here in the middle of the night? *He couldn't have seen it.*

He set off for the village, but two strides away from the boat he remembered that bundle. If it had fallen out of Rose's shopping bag and got caught up in a floating branch, it just might . . . Colin went back. It was definitely wrapped round something, and he was thinking of what Prill had told him, about her passion for "pretty things". She was convinced Rose had taken her doll.

He unrolled layer after sodden layer, dropping what looked like old tights and tea towels in a heap beside him. At last he held it in his hands and saw that his hunch was right. It was the little French "Miss" Grandma had given Prill on her tenth birthday.

The doll was her prize possession, but he'd never liked it. He was irritated by its pert rosebud mouth and its pink-and-white cheeks. It had lost its shoes in the lake and its flounced dress was a rag, but the face was perfect still, almost fresher than before.

As he stared at it the moon sailed out again from the knot of trees above Pit Farm. Amy was as clear as day in his hands, but there were no pouting lips or silly wide-awake eyes looking up at him now. The doll's mouth was a twisted leer, and its eyes were hard and staring. It was a face with all the humanity sucked out of it and spat away.

With a cry Colin dropped the thing in the mud and felt feverishly in the rags at his feet. Then he found a big stone. With his eyes turned away from the grotesque doll's head he made a small bundle, tying it up with a pair of tights and knotting it again and again, in case the stone fell out and the creature swam after him, back across Blake's Pit. Then he waded up to his knees in the freezing water and flung the thing with all his strength into the middle of the lake.

The big moon peered down as he walked away towards Molly's, not daring to look behind, not knowing what he feared, understanding nothing except the fact that his grand gesture against the Edge family was as useless as telling the sea to stand still.

Throwing the doll into Blake's Pit solved nothing. It had gone for ever now, it would rot in the mud at the bottom of the lake, shackled to its great stone. But the face remained with him, and the familiar shape of Elphins, with Molly's lamp in the top window, did nothing to calm him down.

It didn't really matter how Amy had got into Rose's bag, though it was more than likely that she'd stolen her from Prill's bedroom. That wouldn't be news to Prill, she was already suspicious. But what could he possibly tell her about that awful moment at the pit's edge, when the moon had cleared suddenly and revealed that monstrous grinning face? This was one memory he would have to keep to himself, even if it meant he had to lie and lie. Prill must never know about it, not ever.

His brain was splitting as he climbed into bed; now he had seen everything, the doomed city at the bottom of Blake's Pit, the child's toy bewitched, with its painted innocence turned to evil. Under everything the black lake brooded, with its cargo of dead souls, and the dark hump of the farmhouse crouched on the slope above, sleeping but not sleeping.

The bed was warm enough, but he didn't doze off again. He was still awake when the dawn came, thinking about the Edges, about the curse that was upon Stang, and of that terrible face.

# Chapter Thirteen

At ten o'clock he faced Oliver across the kitchen table. "I suppose you're going to say I dreamt it all" he said, in an embarrassed voice. His cousin didn't speak for several minutes, he just sat there, staring into space, but methodically sifting through all the pieces of evidence now stored in his brain. Perhaps it was time to show Colin his photograph again, perhaps he'd see more in it now this had happened. But Oliver was always very cautious, and he didn't want to say anything till he was sure of his case.

"I don't know if you dreamt it or not," he said at last. "And I don't think it matters actually. Dreams can be very important sometimes, they're like visions, spelling out the future. It's in the Bible, of course. My mother believes in dreams."

It was hard to picture Aunt Phyllis dreaming about anything more exciting than school name tapes, or making a good Victoria sponge. What would she make of Stang, with its crazy Mummers, and its horse's head stewing in a pot?

Colin wanted to get out of Elphins today, and right away from Stang. Prill had gone riding, and Molly was out too, with Rose. She wasn't going to let her out of her sight till the Massey business was cleared up. She'd left them a note under the brass candlestick on the kitchen dresser. One of the poodles was missing, the crazy one which kept going into hiding. "Not in the studio when I came down this morning," it said.

"Come on, let's go for a walk," he said to Oliver. "The dogs need a good run, and we might find Dotty. They all get on better now, have you noticed?" Oliver wasn't really listening. He didn't like dogs, and their new "improved" behaviour didn't interest him very much. There were more important things to think about now.

But the missing poodle mattered to Colin, and he was just a little suspicious of the Edges who kept pushing notes of complaint about the dogs barking, through Molly's letter box. She'd laughed and screwed them up to make the fire, but he felt uneasy, even so. He just might take a peep round the shop this morning; it was closed because of Ranswick market day.

Jackie Bostock was having a day off, to go riding with Prill. Molly drove away from the vet's surgery with Rose sitting beside her, well wrapped up. They were going to pay a visit to Aunt Elsie Dutton, a private one, with no police around to make the girl nervous. Molly was determined to make her own enquiries about what Rose had been doing.

She chatted away to her as they rattled down the road to Brereton Cross. "You know, I expect that wretched dog's in the airing cupboard again, dear. It's her favourite hidey-hole at the moment, and I never thought of checking in there. I bet that's where she is." It was the most obvious place too. Molly was getting more and more forgetful these days, and it was beginning to worry her. "Good thing my head's screwed to my shoulders, Rose," she said cheerfully. "I might leave it behind otherwise."

Rose didn't answer. She adored Molly, but she wished they didn't have to go all the way back to Aunt Elsie's. There was Tony's costume to finish for tonight's rehearsal, she wanted to go home and get on with that. She just couldn't understand what all the fuss was about. She'd kept telling the policemen about going to clean up for Aunt Elsie Dutton, and they'd checked her story and told Molly Yes, it was just as she'd said. She could remember the baffled expression of the man in charge quite clearly. "Beats me, missus," he'd said, in the kitchen at Elphins. He'd had three pieces of that new fruit cake.

107

In the end, Molly rather regretted going to quiz Aunt Elsie. They'd woken her up from a nap, and she was cross. The old lady only repeated what Rose had said already, and what the police had written down. The girl wasn't very bright, but she was honest, and all the time that child was missing she'd been here in Brereton Cross. "And if them police come bothering me again, I'll give them what for," she said vehemently, as Molly drove away.

Oliver sat at the kitchen table, busily writing in a notebook. "How long are you going to be?" Colin asked, pulling his anorak on. "Only it's not going to stay fine all day."

"I want to finish this," Oliver muttered, not even lifting his eyes from the paper.

"What is it?"

"Oh, just a few notes." He sounded shifty. "A sort of journal." As he said this, he curved his left hand round the exercise book, just in case Colin tried to read the writing upsidedown. His "Stang file" was strictly private, there were too many loose ends and unanswered questions to let anyone see it yet. Oliver was secretive; he might well never share it with anyone.

The gesture infuriated Colin. That's what little kids did in nursery school, in case anyone "copied". *Honestly*.

"I'll go and post Prill's letter to Mum and Dad," he said curtly. "They empty the box at eleven. Will you be ready when I get back?"

"I might be, if you'll let me get on," Oliver replied, equally curt.

The post box was in the wall opposite Edges' Stores. Colin dropped the letter in, then looked round. The village was quiet, most people must have gone in to Ranswick, to the market. It was the day Harold and Frank went off to a big cash-and-carry place to buy in supplies for the shop, according to Molly. There was nothing doing at the Masseys' either, the curtains were pulled back but there were no other signs of life, and the car had gone from the drive.

Colin crept round to the back of the butcher's shop. The jumble of decrepit sheds was dead and deserted, and there were no lights on. He stuck his nose through the same knothole through which Prill had seen them boiling the head, but it was dark inside. The smell was still around though, still bad enough to turn his stomach over. Poor Prill.

He went up to the back door and tried the handle. It was shut, but not locked. He listened very carefully and then glanced up at the flat above. A window was open, and moth-eaten curtains were blowing in the wind, but the old blue delivery van had gone from its muddy parking place. He went in very cautiously even so, and kept looking round.

Behind the shop there was a big storage area lined with cupboards, and a couple of ancient meat chillers. He stood in the middle of the grubby floor, peering round and straining his ears for the smallest noise. He felt he was being watched, that same cold feeling that had followed him up the lane to Stang church was creeping over him now. Jessie had been whole then, like a puppy, barking with the sheer joy of being alive, dragging him along. But the accident had knocked all the stuffing out of her, and she drooped around now. According to Jimmy Bostock, she might always limp. Colin hated the Edges for that.

The uneven floor was dirty but bare, and there was no sign of Dotty. He looked in vain for her little red collar and her mangled rubber ball. Prill had told him they'd hung William's tail on a hook in that big shed. There were hooks here too, and he wouldn't put it past the Edges to use the dog's hair or tail for one of their horrible Mumming costumes. He was more and more certain that the poodle's disappearance was something to do with them.

But if so, where was she? A squeaky little noise made him spin round, and he thought he might have found her. But it was only the noise of a door moving over a rusty hinge. One of the chillers was open just a crack, and a mouldy, stale, school-dinner smell seeped out of it and into his nostrils. The thick white door was rusty and dark with stains. Colin looked at it in disgust. The Edges couldn't look after anything properly.

That was it though; the longer he stared at the old meat safe the stronger his conviction grew that the silly creature was inside. He walked up to it and peeped in; there was a dim light on, and he saw Easter turkeys swinging from hooks, like so many hats, and rabbits hanging upside down, dripping blood on to the dirty floor.

Colin went in, his determination hardening and turning into rage. He would find the poodle if he looked carefully enough, and he would confront the Edges with it. Before that though, he'd tell the police.

But he hadn't taken two steps into the gloom before the rusty door swung to behind him and chunked solidly into place. Blindly he staggered backwards, with cold feathers swinging in his face, feeling for an inside handle. There must be one, shop fridges were supposed to have them in case of accidents.

*Accidents*? Someone had crept up behind and shut him in. "Serve you right for prying,"—he could just hear Sid Edge's thin sneer. But Sid was at school, and his uncles were at the cash-and-carry. How long would it be before someone came and opened the door?

He stretched out an arm and touched one of the rabbits; the little body was stiff and cold to his fingers, and he shrank away, feeling terribly sick. Terror was growing inside him, it would burst out soon in a great scream. But nobody would hear him behind that door. Panic killed people; he must pull himself together and think.

110

He looked all round carefully. It wasn't a fridge, it was a safe. But it was cold enough. The reddish light was weak and softened the joints on hooks above him into shapeless lumps, but he could see a whole pig's head with the eyes still in it, and the necks of the turkeys, wrung out like pink elastic, had little glittering eyes in them that jewelled the dimness.

He'd once read of a small boy who'd been trapped like this. He'd saved himself by snuggling down in a heap of game birds, pheasants and partridges, anything with feathers, anything that would provide insulation from the cold and keep his blood flowing. There was nothing else to do.

Very slowly, his flesh creeping, Colin reached up and started to unhook the furred and feathered corpses that swung silently above his head. He must make himself a blanket of them and lie underneath. It might be hours before someone came.


Oliver was puzzled when Colin didn't come back. He reread his "Stang file", making a few corrections and adding bits here and there, then he wrote a letter home. It was chilly in the kitchen. Last night's ashes still lay in the fire grate and the hearth was unswept. Rose usually did the fire first thing, but she'd got up late today, and Molly had rushed out without thinking about it.

His hands and feet were freezing, and he decided that it might actually be rather warmer outside. He would wander up the village and look for Colin, but he'd have to wrap up well. He went upstairs to look for his thick walking socks. They'd got muddy and wet a couple of days ago, and Rose had washed them for him. She was a compulsive airer and ironer of clothes, the only person he knew who ironed socks and underpants, apart from his mother.

It was about all they had in common though. Aunt Phyllis wouldn't approve of Rose Salt's odd habits, or of her peculiar disappearing tricks; she liked people she could put into categories, straightforward people that she thoroughly understood. Eccentricity annoyed her, which was why it was very odd that he'd ever been sent to stay with Molly Bover in the first place. If his mother had realized how vague and forgetful she was growing, she'd never have let him come.

His socks were probably airing on the hot-water tank, inside the bathroom cupboard. When he opened the door a furry black bundle leapt out at him, clawing and barking, and seconds later Dotty had torn down the stairs and was rushing manically round the kitchen, snuffling hungrily at her food dish which the systematic Jessie had already licked clean. Oliver extracted his socks, pulled them on, and clumped back down the stairs. The poodle was now scratching at the front door. She must have been fast asleep in that airing cupboard for several hours, the silly creature.

Oliver let her into the garden for a minute, and stood on the step, staring down the path. The tangled garden was curiously still, with daffodils furled up inside their long green hoods and the fruit tree by the gate barely in blossom. Stang was dead. In its rottenness the place reminded him of a fairy tale his mother had once read him, a long time ago, a story of a cold white land always covered with snow, in the power of a wicked witch, a land where it was always winter and never Christmas. He'd always remembered that.

This valley was the same. The sullen, cold spring was dragging on and on, but nothing was really stirring. There was no feeling here of joyous new life. It would always be spring in Stang, but a cold, unwilling one, and he felt that Easter, with all its hope and happiness, would never come.

At twelve o'clock he decided to go out. He wrapped up carefully—anorak, scarf, woolly hat and shut the three dogs in the kitchen. They were furious and hurled themselves noisily against the door, but Oliver took no notice. He was going to visit Winnie Webster, Colin might have wandered up there. "Shut up!" he yelled at them as he locked the door. *Dogs*.

He posted his letter home then crossed the road to Edges' Stores, where he crouched down and peered through a hole in the tatty blind, hoping for a glimpse of the horse's head. Oliver would never have admitted it to the others but he was rather fascinated by Old Hob, and quite jealous of Prill for seeing the whole thing. Why couldn't it have been him?

It was dark on the other side of the hole, so he looked through the letter box. A stale meaty smell wafted through it, and he could hear something, a faint noise coming from somewhere in the back, odd bursts of sound, suppressed cries, like someone screaming through a gag. He knelt on the pavement and put his ear to the slit. The noise had now been replaced by a thin tapping.

He stayed there for several minutes, listening very carefully, and only straightening up again when he was quite certain. His mother had never allowed him to join the boy scouts, she said he wasn't strong enough for all those rough games, and camping, but his father had taught him Morse code.

And any fool knew what was being tapped out in there, by someone locked in presumably, somewhere in Edges' shop. S.O.S.; May Day; Save Our Souls. *Help*.

When Oliver pulled open the door of the chiller, Colin fell out, and went for him like a maniac, with a rusty hook in his hand. The face above the neat green anorak wasn't Oliver's at all, it belonged to the Edges, and it was trying to kill him.

He'd been less than two hours in that dreadful cupboard, stuffed with its dead animals and birds, but it had felt like eternity and he'd lost all sense of time. All he'd been able to think about was Stang's family of madmen, that crazy gang hell-bent on trickery and destruction. All faces were theirs now.

113

Oliver's priggish behaviour often irritated Colin and Prill, but he was at his best in a moment of crisis, and he didn't lose his head now. He grabbed Colin's hand and forced him to drop the meat hook, then he made him sit on the floor and rammed his head between his knees. "I know it was Sid. I'll *kill* him."

"Don't be ridiculous, he's at school. I saw him this morning, getting on the bus." Oliver found an old stool and made him sit on it, then he took off his anorak, scarf and hat, and forced Colin into them.

"This is too tight, Oll, I can't breathe," he stammered, unable to get his words out because of the great waves of cold that were now rippling through him.

"Just put it round you then, you look awful. You've got to warm up. Come on, let's go home and I'll make you a hot drink."

"Wait a minute. I don't think I can walk that far, not yet. Just let me get my breath back, Oliver, I feel a bit peculiar."

Colin was shaking and grey-green, but Oliver had left him for a minute, to inspect the floor of the storeroom. "You know, you can't blame the Edges for this," he said. "Look at these tiles. They're terribly uneven. That's why they use these things." He held up a rough wooden wedge. "They obviously keep the door open with this, when they're putting stuff inside. You must have dislodged it."

"It was *behind* me, you fool," Colin hissed. "Don't you understand? The door was *behind* me, and it swung *open*. How could it swing shut again? Be reasonable."

Oliver didn't say any more because his cousin had tears in his eyes, and he'd never seen that before. Colin must have been horribly frightened inside that chiller. It certainly wasn't the right moment to tell him that the wretched poodle was safe and well inside Molly's studio. But they had to consider everything, all the possibilities; what had happened could easily have been accidental.

114

Little kids were always crawling into old freezers, on dumps and things, and getting trapped.

Colin didn't always think ahead, it had been the same up at Stang churchyard. No wonder the dog had been injured. Builders' yards were dangerous places, like farms, and fridges were the same category. But it was no use telling Colin he'd imagined it all, not at the moment anyway, and especially not after that nightmare about Blake's Pit.

Oliver helped him to his feet and they walked round cautiously to the front of the shop. The coast was still clear, so he guided his shivering cousin across the road and up Molly's path. He wouldn't say anything else now, but it might never have happened if Colin had thought about what he was doing. He was still going on and on about the Edges, but that was silly. In Oliver's opinion there were enough strange things going on in this village anyway, without imagining more.

# Chapter Fourteen

Colin was determined to go to the play rehearsal and tackle the Edges, but he didn't tell Oliver, who obviously thought it was his own fault that he'd got shut in that fridge. He simply took himself off to bed again with a hot drink and two hot-water bottles. He needed a few hours' sleep before facing Tony and Sid.

He just couldn't stop thinking about that family and the fact that they'd not been responsible for the dog's disappearance made no difference whatever. The more he suspected and feared them, the more they fascinated him. He was going to take some photos at the rehearsal, for the school's summer competition. Some good pictures of Stang Mummers would be a real "coup". It would annoy the Edges, but that was part of his plan.

They went across to the schoolroom early, to get a seat at the front. Molly didn't know what had happened in the shop yet—they'd just started to tell her when the phone rang with a message from Blake's End to say Kath Brierley had taken a turn for the worse, and she'd had to rush off. Prill was still at the Bostocks', having supper and hoping she'd be asked to stay the night. "Don't you mind missing the rehearsal?" Jackie said enviously. "Not many people are allowed in on that, you know." Prill concentrated on her apple pie and didn't answer. She couldn't care less any more.

At the beginning of the rehearsal Winnie made an announcement. She wasn't very tall so she climbed on a desk and clapped her hands to call everyone to order. "Before we start," she said rather nervously, "I have to tell you that Mr Massey will not be playing King George.

After what's happened the family is naturally extremely, ah, upset. They have left the village for a while."

Self-satisfied, knowing looks were exchanged between Harold and Frank Edge, and Sid's family glanced at one another slyly. They'd done it, they'd got rid of George Massey. He was an outsider anyway, much too full of himself, and the Council should never have allowed him to build that new house slap-bang in the middle of the village. It was a real eye-sore. He'd already been spotted in Ranswick, going into an estate agent's office. The "For Sale" notices were only a matter of time.

A squabble began about rearranging the main parts. Now King George was missing there was a big hole in the play, but he couldn't be written out. Harold, Frank and Jack got in a huddle with Winnie while everything round them lapsed into chaos. The Puddings organized a sliding competition up and down the room, while the old villagers looked on with frosty disapproval. Oliver pulled a face at Colin and waited for fireworks. Harold Edge was getting very agitated.

In the middle of it all, Rose Salt slid in at the back with Tony's costume. It was still only tacked together but the embroidered horse on the front was finished, an elegant, prancing colt, gold silk against rich purple. "That's beautiful, Rose," Oliver whispered. "You are clever."

Rose annoyed Tony by pulling at his jacket. "Here you are, Tone," she whispered. "I've only got to run it up on the machine now. Why don't you try it on?" Tony Edge was preening himself in the middle of a few admirers, and looked distinctly embarrassed. "Give over, Rose Salt," he muttered. But she wouldn't take the hint, she just stood there goggling at him, with her mouth open, holding out the costume.

"Now come on, Tony," barked Winnie. "Let's have a look at you, then we can get on. We've not got all night. You've done it beautifully, Rose." With foul grumblings Tony Edge pulled the costume over his head. "Stop

117

meithering me then, will you? *Ouch*, it's got pins in, this has. There. Satisfied, are you?"

He looked wonderful in his purple robe; the girls round him stared in admiration, and someone wolf-whistled at the back. But as soon as Rose Salt had got him inside the costume she seemed to want it back again. She began making odd little complaining noises, and pulling at it.

People started to laugh. Rose Salt was a nutter, it was obvious that something didn't please her about the costume. It was hard to believe she'd had a ducking in Blake's Pit only twenty-four hours ago and that she'd been questioned by the police about Posie Massey's disappearance. She was in full cry again now, and determined to get what she wanted. Tony had been enjoying all the attention, but the more he tried to shove her away the more persistent she became. "I want it back, Tone," she kept saying in her shrill, high voice. "Give it back, will you."

Oliver was watching Rose closely. He could see she was frightened and he thought it was something to do with that little gold horse. As soon as she'd seen it, flattened out against Tony's manly chest, the strange little creature had started to worry and complain. She'd been all right until then.

He saw Tony Edge tear the robe off and fling it at her across the floor; he saw her gather it up and push her way to the exit, and he saw her crying. Oliver was torn. He very much wanted to go with her, to find out what was wrong, but he couldn't leave the rehearsal now. Events had just taken a vital turn.

Winnie couldn't get the Mummers to agree about anything. The only person willing to co-operate was Porky Bover, but she wouldn't let him swap parts, he was too good and the only person willing to play a woman. Frank Edge had his hands full with three separate parts and the charge of Old Hob, and Harold would play nothing but the Doctor. "I always have and I always will," he repeated

118

monotonously. "Honestly," sniggered Oliver. "He's just like a record stuck in a groove?

Colin was carefully adjusting his camera; he'd taken three pictures already. There'd been a few dirty looks, but Winnie was there so nobody had told him to stop. Tony had been standing sideways on but he'd been in his purple costume, and the butcher brothers might come out rather well, one in bright orange, one in black, with the strange slit-eyed masks draped over their arms.

There had been several opportunities to approach Sid and Tony, the rehearsal still hadn't begun and they were muttering together in a corner. But Colin couldn't get himself over to them somehow. He wasn't being cowardly but every time he made a move they shot an icy stare at him as if to say "Go on, just you dare." It was uncanny, like two magnets repelling each other, unable ever to touch, or as if Porky's fairy ring had swept a charmed circle round them, keeping intruders away.

"Look," Winnie shrieked suddenly, as Colin dithered on his bench, "Do you want a play or don't you? We've been here forty-five minutes already. King George is one of the key parts and we can't get rid of him, some of the others yes, but not *him*. Now will somebody make a practical suggestion please, or I'm off." And she picked up her handbag and her sensible raincoat.

"I'll have a go," Oliver piped up suddenly in his reedy voice. Colin stared at him in disbelief, and there was an awful silence in the schoolroom. Had he gone stark raving mad?

"*YOU*?" Harold, Frank and Jack said together.

"Yes, *me*," Oliver said firmly. "No one else has offered."

The Edges looked at each other. How dare he? He was an outsider, with his posh southern accent and his clever little smile. What could he be thinking of? But Oliver knew the play by heart because he'd picked up a copy of the lines at the first rehearsal. He'd got an excellent memory and it hadn't taken him very long. "I think I could do it," he said, "I've been in plays at school." But his voice wavered slightly. Jack Edge was glowering at him, and he looked so fierce and hairy.

The three brothers stood in a line, looking down at Oliver's pale blue eyes and his spindly legs. He was knee-high to a grasshopper. "You're an outsider," Jack growled. "It won't work. You're not from round here."

"Well, George Massey wasn't, and he was in it," Oliver retorted.

"Yes, and look what happened to him," Frank said loudly. "His garage went up in smoke, and his kid nearly got herself drowned. That's what happens if you go changing everything. We should never have let him be in it." But from the back there were loud cries of "Shame!" and "Rubbish!" and "Give the lad a chance!"

Oliver took courage from all this and stood up. "My name's Wright," he said. "That's something, and my father used to live in Stang—you ask Molly Bover. King George is always played by a Wright and I could—"

"Shut your big mouth," Harold Edge bellowed. "You're an *adopted* child, it's not the same at all."

Oliver turned scarlet, then white. Colin thought he was going to pass out. For a second all the things his mother had said to reassure him, flew out of his head. ("We *chose* you, Oliver. We were lucky.") Everyone in the hall was staring at him, and some were tittering. He could have killed Harold Edge.

"Look, Tony can have a go at the King," Winnie said suddenly, putting her hand on Oliver's shoulder. She'd become quite fond of him, she liked clever children. But it wouldn't do, of course. How odd of him to suggest it. Tony wasn't much of an actor but at least he looked the part, and he had a very loud voice. "Sid," she went on. "You can be Slasher, you've got a good memory so it shouldn't take you long to learn. It's a pity you're not a bit bigger," she added tactlessly, "but there we are."

120

Sid didn't even hear the last remark. He was delighted to be given Slasher because the play always ended with a great big fight between him and King George. He'd enjoy having a bash at Tony. Jason Edge, a cousin who lived in the caravan, was roped in to be Little Devil Doubt. It was the perfect part for him, Winnie decided privately. He was the village tearaway, given to shoving heads down school lavatories and spitting at people from on top of walls. Oh, the *Edges*. They'd shortened her life by about ten years.

Colin stayed for the whole rehearsal, taking more photographs, but Oliver slipped away. He went straight up to his bedroom at Elphins and shut the door. He didn't want to speak to anyone for the rest of the evening.

He'd tried. It was a crazy thing to do, but he'd tried, because he was seeing things more clearly now. Tony Edge wouldn't do in the role of King George, it ought to be a Wright, and with "Dear Noel" sunning himself in Florida, Oliver thought they'd have seen the sense in his taking over. They were really very stupid if they thought that the village stranglehold on the play was enough, and that any old Edge or Bover would do in the King's part. It went deeper than that.

It was the Edges themselves who'd gone on to Winnie about "breaking the luck" and about not changing the old pattern. Well, patterns were more complicated than they realised. It was quite obvious to Oliver.

When Colin left the schoolroom he saw a familiar car making its way along the village street from the direction of Blake's End. It belonged to Christopher Eliot, the elderly doctor who'd been looking after Miss Brierley. Molly was already home, staring into the kitchen fire with a hollow-eyed, blank look that was becoming rather familiar. The old lady had died at nine that night.

He found Prill in the sitting-room watching T.V. with Rose. Molly went off into the studio with the dogs and shut the door. She was very silent but she'd left a hot supper ready for them, and she was as kind as ever.

After the rehearsal a group of Mummers in full costume went racketing round the village with Old Hob, kicking milk bottles over and making dogs bark. They were still at it after midnight. Molly was late in bed again. She slammed her bedroom window shut and pulled the curtains across quite viciously. Tony Edge's raucous bellows were too much for her tonight.

Her best and oldest friend was dead. There had been Brierleys in Stang for two hundred years, and her friend Kath was the last. She'd never married, and her brother Wilfred had had a family of girls. Kath was the last of the line and the name had died with her.

It was the breaking of one pattern that the Edges neither cried about nor understood. They didn't have friends, they simply stuck together like glue, and as thick as thieves.

As she climbed into bed Molly heard Oliver coughing in the room next door. That child worried her. Winnie Webster had been on the phone earlier that evening to report that he'd managed to upset the Edges—he'd wanted to be in the play or something. Perhaps now the Masseys had gone everything might calm down a bit, but she didn't feel very convinced about it. She still wondered about these three children and their role in things, especially Oliver's. That boy was wise beyond his years and although he was the quietest of them all she felt he was a disturbing influence somehow.

She fell asleep thinking about the old days, and about Kath Brierley. She'd known Molly all her life, she'd even taught her in Sunday School, more than sixty years ago. Death had come to the village tonight, and the saying round here was that it never came alone. Its victim was old and tired, and she'd been ill for a long time now. But it was still death.

# Chapter Fifteen

Two days later Molly set her alarm to go off earlier than usual, and got up while Rose and the three children were still asleep. She was going to do a "firing" and she hadn't quite finished packing the shelves of the kiln. It was a tricky operation, especially with her unsteady, arthritic hands, and she needed peace and quiet to concentrate.

Stang was unusually quiet. The Easter holidays had started at last so there would be no chattering schoolchildren hanging about on the green, waiting for the early bus into Ranswick. It would be some time before they shook themselves awake this morning and began careering round the village on bikes. Oddly enough, though, Sid Edge was already up and about, lolling against the window of his uncles' shop and looking up and down the street. He was no doubt waiting for a victim to come along to be shown the wonders of his brand-new racer. There couldn't be any other reason for getting up so early, Molly decided. It was his birthday on Saturday, she remembered, the same day they were going to bury Kath Brierley. Not that an old woman's funeral would interest the Edges.

She was watching Sid from the front parlour window, and she noticed that he kept glancing across at the house. All the Edges had this nasty habit of spying, and she'd never really got used to it, not after fifty years of living in Stang. She waited till he was looking along the street again, then dropped the window curtain. She didn't intend to give him any information whatever about her activities.

As she went back into the flagged hall she suddenly thought of something and walked to the front door, clicking her tongue with annoyance. One of the poodles had gone missing yet again, yesterday morning; it was Dotty of course, and this time she hadn't been shut in the airing cupboard, or anywhere else in the house. The children had hunted all over the village, but there'd been no sign of her, and they'd gone to bed last night with the dog still missing.

Molly half wished she'd not been so soft-hearted about these poodles. They were expensive to feed, Dotty was a real nuisance, and the pair of them made far too much noise. She just hoped the wretched dog hadn't been hanging round the back of Edges' shop again. Last time that had happened Harold had knocked on her door to complain, with the hapless poodle stuffed under one arm like a joint of pork.

She put her hand on the front door bolt, then dropped it again. She really didn't want to get into a conversation with Sid Edge just at that moment. She went through to the kitchen and opened the back door instead. The two remaining dogs slipped past her legs and into the damp back garden, and Molly called quietly, "Dotty! Dotty! Silly dog, where on earth are you?" She listened, and waited, but all was silence. After a few minutes, Jessie and Potty trotted in again and hung round her feet, hopefully waiting for signs of breakfast, but Molly's mind was back on the kiln.

"I must check what's gone in," she said to herself, shuffling round in her old slippers, making herself a mug of tea. "That bread crock's my main problem, a waste of space really. Still, perhaps this time . . ." She often chatted to herself as she pottered about. "I'm a good listener," she told Rose who, for all her odd ways, thought talking to yourself was an eccentric habit. The bread crock was a large item ordered specially by a lady in Ranswick, and Molly had made two attempts at it already. Large pots were often tricky, and both had shattered during the firing. "Third time lucky," she told herself, opening the studio door; when you fired a kiln all sorts of things could go wrong.

124

In the studio she discovered that the kiln door was shut already, and the main switch was down. For a second or two the facts didn't really sink in. Molly simply stood there, staring at the kiln across the dusty flagstones, with the blue mug in her hand and her mouth half open. Then, quite calmly, and willing herself not to panic, she walked slowly into the middle of the cluttered room and looked round carefully, counting, estimating, racking her brains to try and remember just what she had done the day before.

She had no recollection at all of packing the kiln, or of switching it on. True, she was forgetful these days, but she wasn't *so* far gone, not yet anyway. Besides, there on a shelf behind her was Mrs Warburton's unfired breadcrock, and half a dozen large coffee cups she'd ordered at the same time. She wouldn't have fired a half-empty kiln. But she'd started to shiver slightly even so, and she put the untouched mug of tea down on a stool.

The kiln was an old one, with the most basic controls. Molly was so familiar with it she could more or less tell by feel how long it had been on, in the early stages. Shakily, she stretched both hands and put them against the door, detecting only the faintest warmth. The needle of the heat gauge, under its cracked glass, had scarcely moved from zero. She reached up to the wall behind and switched the kiln off at the mains, noticing, as she did so, that there was a thin, vapoury cloud coming from the "bung hole" at the top, and an odd, slightly steamy smell in the air.

She must open the door and get it properly cool again before arranging her shelves inside. One of those children must be responsible for this—Oliver was the most likely, he'd been very curious about the whole business of potting, and had trailed round the studio after her yesterday, asking a string of questions. Yet he seemed such a law-abiding child, always asking what they

125

were "allowed" to do—a boy after his mother's own heart. Why on earth interfere with her kiln like this, and at this hour of the morning, too?

She had eased herself down on to her knees in front of the kiln door when a big tongue suddenly licked her face. "*Jessie*, now out you *go*," she protested feebly, but the hungry dog only retreated a few inches and sat quietly by the clay bin, wagging her tail. The poodle was much less obedient. She stood up on her hind legs and buried her sharp little paws in Molly's neck, licking and yapping at the same time, her idiotic pompom tail whirring to and fro like an electric brush. She'd been busy chewing something, but dropped it again in order to lick the unresponsive Molly. It looked like an old library ticket enclosed in a plastic case. Molly picked it up and examined it. Holding it at arm's length she could just about read it without her spectacles; it was a bus pass, and it belonged to Sidney P. Edge of Ranswick Middle School.

Potty was now busy trying to curl up in the sloping lap. She'd stopped barking and started to whine, punctuating the monotonous droning noise with the odd dry yelp. And suddenly, from somewhere far away, Molly heard an answering squeak. The fussing poodle pricked up its ears, loosened its precarious hold on the woman's dressing gown, and dropped to the floor like a big black spider. The tiny squeak came again, and this time Potty leapt up at the kiln door, scrabbling at the chipped paint and hurling herself bodily against it. Jessie limped over and stood interestedly behind Molly, making the occasional low woofling noise.

She almost kicked the two dogs aside in her efforts to pull the door open. It swung out on scraping hinges and she herself thrust her head inside, feeling blindly round with shivering hands.

Dotty was a tiny pulsating heap in the furthest corner of the empty kiln. She was making feeble mewing noises, like a kitten; her head seemed to be stuck lopsidedly between her woolly shoulders, and as Molly pulled her out and set her gently on the floor, her four legs straddled in all directions, as if they didn't belong to her any more. She was smelly and sticky all over. She'd been sick in the kiln, and her black wool was matted and standing up in peaks. Jessie was wary. She stood her distance from the disgusting black object that had now collapsed on the studio floor, and which Molly was coaxing and wrapping in an old towel. But Potty was jubilant, leaping at her legs, and rapturously licking all the mess off her poor sister's ears and nose as she lay all bundled up in green and yellow stripes, being carried round the studio like a baby.

The dog seemed shocked and stunned—something about its glassy, half-lidded stare suggested it might have been drugged. Even so, it would live. It was already squirming back to life inside its striped swaddling clothes, and one beady eye was following the progress of the other dogs up and down the studio floor, while the shattered Molly paced mechanically to and fro, wondering what on earth she should do next, and how in heavens' name this terrible thing had happened.

And suddenly, she knew. In a fit of panic she flung the studio door open, bundled the two dogs into the kitchen and shut them in. Then, still cradling Dotty, she sagged down on to an old chair, looking at the open kiln, the bread crock, and the row of unfired cups on a shelf, with that awful sweaty smell in her nostrils. She knew what must have happened now, earlier this morning, and what had been *meant* to happen. And if she hadn't set her alarm and got up so early, the wretched poodle . . .

Molly dug down in her pocket for the bus pass. Anyone else who'd tried to pull off a bizarre trick like this would have put the length of the village between himself and the scene of the crime, or else got on that bicycle and made himself scarce for the rest of the day. Not Sidney P. Edge, oh no, he was actually hanging round the house to see what came of his spectacular "arrangements". He might still be out there, propping up the fence and staring at Elphins with those hard, suspicious little eyes.

The dog seemed to have fallen into a doze. Tucking it under her arm in its striped towel, Molly lifted the latch of the outer studio door, slipped into the garden and made her way round the house.

Grateful for her rubber-soled slippers she stole silently down the path and through the front gate. Sure enough, Sid was still outside the shop and bending over his shiny new bike. It was nothing to Molly that she stood in the village street in her dressing gown, with her long grey hair floating in the wind. She marched straight across and grabbed Sid by the shoulder.

He dropped his bicycle pump and whipped round, opening his mouth to protest. But when he saw the wriggling, stripey bundle, and the bus pass thrust under his nose, he let out a weird, strangled shout. Then, to Molly's amazement, he didn't cut and run, he simply collapsed against the wall and stared up at her.

She couldn't quite believe it, she'd been all set for a fight and she'd have dragged him bodily into the house if need be, rather than let him go. But it wasn't necessary; he went back with her into the studio quite meekly and told her everything in one great burst, as if he was glad to get the hideous trick off his conscience.

"They're horrible dogs, miss," he snivelled, with his eyes fixed on the kiln door. "I hate them, everyone does, allus mekkin a row. And that one's the worst, it got me into trouble with Our Vi. It tore one of her dresses up, and she said it was me, doin' a costume for the play like. She gave me a right thumpin'. Well, it came round the shop yesterday, cadgin', and I got it drunk like, on me uncles' home brewed." A smile crept over his pasty little face as he thought of it; making that daft dog tipsy had been dead good.

"*How did it get inside the kiln?*" Molly's voice was unnaturally harsh and shrill, and she felt she was beginning to lose her grip on the situation. The silly dog certainly had a passion for creeping into warm places and going to sleep—Rose was for ever turfing her out of cupboards. Even so, with Harold Edge's beer inside her . . . She gave Sid a long, hard stare, and tightened her grip on his wiry little arm.

"All right, so you got the poor animal drunk yesterday," she said, as if tormenting an innocent creature was the most natural sport in the world. "So that's where it was while those three children were walking their legs off looking for it. And you came into the studio with it this morning, I suppose? Then what did you do?"

Sid hung his head and started to cry, and Molly shook him hard. She couldn't stand much more of this. Her best friend was dead, Rose Salt had been up to her silly disappearing tricks again, and she had these three children on her conscience. They obviously weren't enjoying their holiday at all, and the girl kept writing long letters to her parents. "What did you *do*?" she repeated. "Answer me, will you, or I'll knock your head off."

Sid Edge stared at her wildly. She would, too, she was a mad woman, and if his father got to hear what he'd been up to he'd thrash him within an inch of his life. He didn't know what to say for the best, or what lies to tell.

"I—I don't know what came over me, miss," he blurted out at last. "I was in here with it like, and it was warm. It went up to the kiln and put its nose in, and then . . . it crept in, like. It *wanted* to."

"And you shut the door on it?"

Sid didn't reply. He stared at the floor instead, plotting his next move. It was just his luck to have dropped the bus pass. It must have fallen from his pocket as he reached up in the early-morning gloom, to plug the kiln in. If it hadn't been for that she would never have found out.

129

"So you shut the door on it?" Molly repeated, "And then you switched on? *Answer me, will you!*" And before she could stop herself she had struck him very hard across the face.

Quite suddenly the boy got to his feet. He was cunning, like all the Edges, and he knew his rights. His best policy was silence. If he ignored her questions she couldn't really pin anything on him, not even with the bus pass. "I'm tellin' me mam," he said, rubbing the tears dry and straightening his cap. "I'm goin' straight home and I'm tellin'. You're not supposed to hit children, Mrs Bover."

At that moment it was Molly who felt like a child. The snivelling Sid Edge seemed to grow as he stood in the doorway, and there was a dreadful hardness in his face that made her cold inside. But for all their craftiness the ferret eyes were plainly bewildered. "I don't know what came over me, miss," was what she always remembered whenever she thought about their extraordinary conversation, and she could picture him quite clearly, sitting on the old chair, watching with mild fascination as the wretched dog crept up to the kiln door, letting it go inside to its own death.

Sid had stepped into the garden. There was a dark red patch on his right cheek, and he was stroking it with filthy fingernails. "I'm goin'," he repeated. "I'm goin' home and I'm tellin'."

"Go then, get out of my sight," Molly spat at him, through clenched teeth, closing her eyes with the weariness of it all. "Your parents'll be hearing from me when Miss Brierley's funeral's out of the way, so you can tell them what you like. I know you've been in here, tampering with all my stuff, and I know what you've been up to. You need a psychiatrist, Sid Edge."

She shut her back door, bolted it, then sat down again. The two dogs scratched at the kitchen door, puzzled by the non-appearance of breakfast, But Molly Bover was miles away. There wasn't a single member of the Edge family for whom she had the least respect, they were trouble-makers and bullies, sly neighbours and dishonest shopkeepers. All who knew them said the same. But this attempt to roast poor Dotty was the sickest thing any of them had ever attempted.

She might walk up to Winnie's later and ask her about Sid Edge; she'd taught him in the village school and she'd know if he had any "problems". Molly really did wonder whether a boy like that ought to see a doctor. He must have had some kind of brainstorm. What else could you say about a kid who got a dog drunk on home-made beer, then shut it in an oven?

When he heard her coming back towards the kitchen, Oliver busied himself over the fire. He'd been eavesdropping again, and this time he'd heard everything, even the bit about Sid needing to see a psychiatrist. The pathetic little creature must have been curled up inside the kiln, fuddled with beer and dead to the world, when suddenly . . . Sid Edge . . . It could so easily have been turned to a little heap of ash.

Oliver shuddered. What twisted thinking could prompt anyone to do a thing like that? A brain that dreamed up such a trick must be horribly unbalanced, if not insane. He went outside to empty the ash bucket and met Molly in the rear passage with the shivering poodle in her arms. She didn't comment on his dressing gown, or on the fact that he was helpfully laying the fire at seven in the morning. She just said, "Oh, hello, Oliver," in a tight kind of voice, and he heard her slamming the kettle down on to the stove.

The ash bin was full of purple cloth, singed brown by flames. Rose Salt had come in from the play rehearsal, pulled Tony's Slasher costume apart, and tried to burn it. Molly, stunned by the news of Kath Brierley, and sitting on her own in the dark kitchen had only realized what was happening when the thing was half consumed. She didn't know what it was but it could easily set the chimney alight.

She'd thrown water on the fire and later stuffed everything in the bin. Rose Salt had been packed off to bed; Molly was in no mood for her just then.

Oliver was just going to empty his ash over the charred remnants when something caught his eye, something that shone. He put down his bucket, reached down and pulled it out. It was the little gold horse Rose had made for the front of Tony's costume, on a scrap of purple cloth now only about ten inches square. Miraculously, the fire had puttered and died without touching it.

He had a good look at it. Rose ought to go to art college, not stay at Elphins, washing floors; the horse was beautiful. Embroidery could make pictures heavy and lifeless but this little creature had all the grace and elegance of an artist's drawing.

But as he stared at it a coldness crept over Oliver, striking through his winceyette pyjamas and his warm dressing gown, sending shudders down his backbone. For a split second the prancing colt had looked like something else, no longer a little horse in arched profile, but a thing with a face. He was aware of its burning, heavy stare, and of a darkness in its eyes that came up and hit him like a fist.

His eyes were watering as he stood in the damp garden by the row of dustbins, and he groped in his pocket for his spectacles. But they were up in the bedroom, on top of his "Stang file". Inside that notebook was an account of all that had happened since they'd come to Molly's, and his photo of the hedge with the "bird" in it. He blinked and gazed more steadily. The scrap of gold embroidery was a horse again, but the icy coldness was still there inside him, and he remembered Rose's terror at the play rehearsal, and her tears as she pushed her way through the tittering villagers.

What had she seen? And what had Colin seen in that awful nightmare? It may well have been a dream, but you couldn't ignore it, nor what had happened inside Edges'

132

shop. He'd been wrong to attack Colin for blaming the "accident" on them. They came into everything, even when they were miles away.

Oliver went hurriedly through the kitchen and told Molly he was going to get dressed. The little gold horse was crumpled up in his dressing gown pocket. He ought to destroy it, burn it or fling it into Blake's Pit with Prill's old French doll. It was evil.

The darkness was creeping over them now, like a foul and poisonous mist, like something that seeped under doors and through keyholes, like a shadow that lay in wait, hovering and gathering itself in silence, getting ready to spring. Things were coming to a head.

He spent ages sitting on his bed before getting dressed. A whole hour later Colin opened one eye and saw him huddled in his dressing gown, poring over a notebook. "Are you O.K., Oll?" he said. He looked a bit red round the eyes, and as he'd come to, Colin had heard him muttering, "Proof, we must have proof."

"Proof? What of, for heaven's sake? Proof about what, Oliver?"

But there was no answer. Oliver couldn't explain because he couldn't see the whole picture yet, and what he could see he didn't understand. Prill was frightened to death by what was happening in Stang, and Colin had started to have violent nightmares. He wasn't going to show them his picture of the dunnet, or Rose's horse, or tell them about Sid Edge trying to kill the poodle, not yet anyway. But it didn't mean he wasn't going to *do* anything.

Just what had to be done Oliver didn't know yet, but he was becoming more and more certain about one thing. It was all up to him.

# Chapter Sixteen

What happened next couldn't be blamed on the Edges. On the contrary, if they'd not been around it could well have been fatal. It was a good thing Oliver saw it, and not the other two; it would have sent them screaming out of Stang. Living with old people you got used to little accidents. It hadn't been very nice, for example, when Mr Catchpole had fallen down the stairs and split his head open. But that was nothing compared to this.

His two cousins had gone riding. Colin had never been on a horse's back, but he was game to try. Oliver suspected that he wanted to keep an eye on Prill; they were both worried about her, she was so withdrawn and silent now, picking at her food and snapping at everyone. This dank valley, with its silent village and its round black pit lowering down below, had cast a dark shadow over her. Oliver didn't read other people's letters, and only eavesdropped on their phone calls when the need arose, but he knew how desperate she was to get away from Molly's and to go back to her parents and that screaming toddler.

He'd been sent up to collect some cakes from Winnie Webster—not just any old cakes, she informed him, but special fruit buns, always made on the day before Good Friday and distributed to the villagers. It was Winnie's turn to bake them this year. Oliver had to deliver the cakes to Edges' Stores. The Mummers would go round the village with them tonight after their play rehearsal.

He listened patiently while she told him what he'd already found out in the public library. The buns were called "Soul Cakes" and the idea was that you ate them to increase your strength. "Of course, they're supposed to be eaten at Hallowe'en," she said, "when the year's dying. Not in spring. You don't need new life in *spring*, for goodness sake. But this village got it wrong as usual."

Oliver was looking out of the window at Porky Bover fiddling with the new lawn mower. It still didn't feel like spring round here, nothing was growing, and it was a waste of time cutting those lawns. There was no grass to cut. "You're eating the souls of the dead, you see," Winnie went on, beating eggs vigorously and adding currants. "All the dead of the last twelve months. Their strength goes into you, basically. Interesting, isn't it?"

"Well, I suppose it's like being a cannibal," he said thoughtfully. "Or a vampire, sucking someone's blood out." He wasn't squeamish, but he didn't really like discussing this while old Miss Brierley lay stiff and cold at the undertaker's waiting to be buried. He mustn't let Prill hear about the Soul Cakes. She'd throw up.

They were having a cup of tea together and waiting for the buns to cool on their wire racks, when a loud cry from outside took them both to the window and then through the back door. Winnie's neat and tidy lawns all sloped down sharply to her front fence, and Porky Bover was lying near the gate, hanging on to the handles of the new mower. The engine was making a great roaring noise, the blade must still be whizzing round, mangling the turf, and there was a broad skid mark in the grass. It looked as if Porky had been somehow pulled down the hill, as if the machine had suddenly gone out of control, dragging him after it. His right foot was hidden under the mower and his mouth was wide open in a terrible, silent scream.

Oliver had once seen a man's hand crushed in a car door. The pain was so horrific he'd made no noise at all. The boy had never forgotten that surprised, horrified stare, frozen in silent agony, and being Oliver he'd followed up the accident in the local paper. The hand had been amputated in the end.

135

He approached Porky with icy calmness and pulled a red lever to "Off". Then he looked at him. The fat, kindly face was greenish-white, the eyes were two slits, and still he didn't cry out. Behind them, Winnie Webster gave a little moan and sank down in a faint. Oliver rapidly assessed the situation. There were no stones or walls for her to have hit her head on, and she was fortunately very small. He got her under the arms and dragged her across the grass like a sack of potatoes, propping her against the garden fence. Then he went back to Porky. He couldn't put it off any longer, every second counted in a case like this. He must move the mower and find out what had actually happened.

Half-closing his eyes, Oliver lifted it very gingerly off the hidden foot, then he forced himself to look. These things were dangerous, like a lot of machines. They were always issuing warnings about them on the radio.

There was a lot of blood, and three toes were sticking out of the end of the boy's sneaker in a sticky pink bunch. Oliver leaned across to pick a pair of smashed glasses out of the grass, and Porky moaned and gave a little cry. Then a violent spasm jerked him sideways and he started to scream hysterically.

Winnie Webster was coming round and moaning, but Oliver ignored her and ran into the house. He picked up the phone and dialled Molly's number, but it was engaged. Slamming it down and starting to panic, he looked at a list of "useful" phone numbers pinned on the wall. He must dial "999" and hope they didn't get lost this time. But after the first "9" Oliver stopped and dialled another number. "Edge Bros, Butchers and General Store, Ranswick 440". They had a van and they certainly had fridges. If Porky's foot was as bad as it looked they might need ice.

Harold picked up the phone. "Get off the line," he hollered as soon as Oliver had blurted out his message. "And listen, kid, don't try to move him, whatever you do.

Throw a rug or something over him and get one for the old girl too."

But the old girl had perked up and standing over Porky, swaying about. "Have some of this, Miss Webster," said Oliver, giving her a glass of water. "Look, why don't you sit on the bench? Someone's coming. They'll be here in a minute."

Porky Bover's face had gone from green to white. Oliver took off his anorak, rolled it up, and pushed it under his head. "Porky," he whispered, but there was no response. If the boy was breathing, something rather odd was happening, because his chest wasn't going up and down, and Oliver couldn't find a pulse.

The turf under his mangled foot had turned dark red, and all the grass blades were sticking together as the blood slowly clotted. Oliver's stomach heaved. He ran back into the house and picked up the phone again, but someone was using the party line. All he could hear was two women discussing the crimes of a thieving builder called Roland Clutton. He slammed it down and ran through the front door, and down the lane towards Blake's Pit. Harold Edge hadn't turned up yet so he was going to alert the nearest neighbours, even though they were the people at Pit Farm.

"Porky Bover's had an accident with that mower," Oliver said quite casually at tea. "I thought he might."

Prill was sitting by the fire in the little front room. She'd just bitten into a hot crumpet and the butter was dribbling down her chin. She was in a better frame of mind after her day's riding, and her cheeks were glowing after several hours in the fresh air. Colin, on the other hand, had stiff knees and a sore bottom. At the word "accident" his heart missed a beat. Why couldn't Oliver pipe down? He'd had quite a difficult day, trying to humour the moody Prill, and kidding her out of her wild imaginings about Stang. Now everything was going to be wrecked again.

"What kind of accident?" she said, dropping the half-eaten crumpet back on to the plate again.

"Oh, nothing much," Oliver said carefully. "Well, not as it *happened*. Ouch!" Under the table, Colin had just aimed a hefty kick at his ankles and hit the target spot on.

"*What kind of accident, Oliver*?" Prill repeated, in a dangerous voice. That appalling dead feeling was creeping up over her like a dank fog. It had happened again. The village was drawing its terrible net round them, tighter than ever. They would never escape from it, never ever.

"Well it . . . it sort of ran away with him . . ." Oliver started, less confident now as he saw all the colour draining away from Prill's face, and rubbed at his bruised ankle. "And it cut his foot rather badly. They'll have to send the mower back to the manufacturers, I should think. Oh, it was his own *fault*," he lied. Anything to stop Prill going on at him.

But it was Rose who did the real damage, suddenly appearing in the doorway with a plate of warm scones. She knew all the village gossip, and she thought she was doing Oliver a favour, telling the others what was being talked about all over Stang—how he had been the hero of the hour, phoning for the Edges and bringing Winnie round from a faint, running up to Pit Farm and fetching Our Vi back with him to look at Porky, because he thought he was "going". Rose told the story with real pride. She rather admired Oliver.

"And he had to have a blood transfusion," she finished breathlessly. "Two goes they had at him before the doctor said he was all right. His dad and mam were that worried."

The effect of Rose's speech on Prill was quite extraordinary. She had listened to the saga of Porky's foot in silence, but with mounting alarm, and when Rose mentioned the blood transfusion she went into a kind of hysterical fit, throwing herself round the room and crying, and yelling, "There you are! What did I tell you?" while

138

Oliver looked on helplessly, and Colin grabbed her arm, trying to make her sit down again and drink some tea.

Prill pushed cup and plate away from him savagely, and they crashed to the floor. Tut-tutting, the poor, bewildered Rose got down on to her knees and began to pick up the bits of china, muttering darkly to herself and wagging her head sorrowfully. This seemed to madden Prill even more; she was yelling at the top of her voice now "I *told* you we should post that letter. They'll never come for us if they don't know what's going on in this place, now will they? They don't know about Jessie's foot yet, you know, and when they hear about Porky's little *accident* . . ." she screamed shrilly. "I begged you to let me post that letter, Colin, but you said no. Now this has happened. I should never have listened to you."

"Prill. For goodness *sake*," Colin began hopelessly, shooting a look at Oliver who was on his knees by the fire, picking up bits of china. They'd argued about Prill's letter all the way to the riding stables on the bus. It was a desperate plea to her parents, telling them how unhappy she was at Elphins, and how she wanted to go back home.

Colin had persuaded her not to post it, not yet anyway, and it was upstairs, zipped into the front of his anorak. He'd pointed out how hurt Molly would feel, how it would mean his father having to abandon the portrait, and what a disappointment that would be, and all because of them. As they'd jogged down the sunny lanes together, Prill had cheered up considerably. What was happening in Stang had all seemed rather remote and unimportant for a while, receding into the leafy distance.

But this fresh development had turned everything black again. After tomorrow, when they'd booked another riding lesson, Prill would have no money left, and the Bostocks—her lifeline—were going away on holiday. She was *determined* to contact her parents.

Molly collided with her in the doorway. The tinkling of china, and Prill's throaty hysterics, had brought her in from the studio where she'd been privately dosing Dotty. The dog's sojourn in the kiln had obviously upset its insides, and it kept coughing and being sick. "Prill, dear, what on earth's the matter now?" The girl's scarlet, tear-stained face was all screwed-up and ugly. She simply shoved past poor Molly, muttering something about writing a letter, and began to mount the stairs.

Molly peeped into the front parlour. Oliver was still hunting for pieces of china in the hairs of the rug; Colin shrugged and rolled his eyes up to heaven rather comically. "Rose went on a bit about Porky's accident," he said in a low voice. "And Prill didn't like it. She's a bit squeamish, I'm afraid."

"Oh, *Rose*," Molly chided gently, "I wish you hadn't done that. You've upset her, dear, and it may give her nightmares." Up above, Prill's bedroom door slammed loudly and the windows rattled. "As if we'd not got enough to worry about," Molly muttered, going wearily up the stairs and wondering what on earth she could say to the girl. Thank goodness nobody knew about Dotty, anyway.

Colin let her go. He'd had enough of Prill and her alarming changes of mood for one day, and his patience was at an end. Besides, he really must find out more from Oliver, and in particular, just how Porky had got tangled up in that mower. It was only a rotary cutter, like the one they had at home. Could it really have "run away" with Porky, as Oliver had suggested? There was no rhyme or reason to an episode like that.

It was like the stone that had hurtled off the tower, like Posie Massey's inexplicable disappearance. Like the meat safe door that had shut "by itself". Like Prill's doll. Colin was frightened. He must talk to Oliver *now*, while he had the chance, and hear his side of the story.

By seven o'clock Winnie Webster was tucked up in bed with a sedative, and a neighbour had agreed to stay the night. The play rehearsal was cancelled. After Oliver's phone call the Edges had come up trumps. Harold and Frank had torn down to the bungalow in their shabby old van, stowed the senseless Porky in the back like a side of beef, and driven to Ranswick Hospital at seventy. Oliver had found Vi at Pit Farm, all on her own, and she'd come back with him, hammering on the door of the caravan as they ran past to stir the occupants into life.

The mother of the Puddings had caught them up as they turned into Winnie's gate. She'd made gallons of sweet tea while the men got Porky comfortable in the van, and Our Vi had stayed with Winnie long after everyone else had gone, sitting quietly at her side and stroking her hand, because the poor woman couldn't stop shaking.

In the end Oliver had crept away. His brain was working overtime and he had a splitting headache. Everything had moved on to a different plain now. The Edges still frightened him, and he still hated that dreadful staring look they all had, even Our Vi, who was incapable of adding two and two, according to the heartless Winnie.

The most terrifying thing was their kindness to Porky. If they had somehow brought these terrible things to pass why had they all helped him, Oliver wondered? Why hadn't they passed by on the other side, and laughed?

Molly spent ages upstairs with Prill and they eventually came down together, the best of friends, and took the three dogs out for a long walk. Prill hardly said a word to anyone for the rest of the day, and she looked very tearful and red-eyed, but at least she didn't snap.

Later that night they were all playing Monopoly round the kitchen table when there was a loud banging on the front door. "Da didee Da Da," very slow and deliberate. "It's the Mummers," Molly said quietly. "Come on,

Rose. Open the door and let's get it over with. We'll all come."

Before Rose was halfway down the hall the knocker was banged again. When at last she opened the door they saw a dark knot of figures filling the narrow path, giggling and pushing at each other, with more people behind them in the shadows. Everyone was in costume, and most of the Mummers wore curious slit-eyed hoods. Some of the children had plastic horror masks looped behind their ears,—skulls, and were-wolves, and grinning vampires. Rose stepped back a few inches.

"Come on, Jason," someone shouted. "Get to the front, will you, we've not got all night."

A small figure, dressed all in red, with a fat forked tail, was pushed from the back and forced on to the doorstep. "Do your stuff, Jase," Sid Edge shouted.

"Tony looks nice," Rose whispered to Prill, as little Devil Doubt made a great show of clearing his throat.

Bashfully Jason Edge held out a paper plate with five fruit buns on it. "Cakes for your dame, and Cakes for your squire, and Cakes for the stranger who sits by your fire," he mumbled. Then, "Here you all are."

Rose stood dithering on the step. Tony's new costume wasn't as nice as hers, she was thinking wistfully. Vi had made it and she was a real codger with a needle. "Take them, *take* them," Molly was hissing in her ear. "It's cold out here, I want to lock up." But before Rose could take the floppy plate Tony Edge had shoved forwards from the back. "Old Hob, Old Hob, Give him a tanner, Give him a bob," he yelled, and old William's huge skull, majestic with its bells and ribbons and flowing silk streamers, was thrust at them all in turn, with its jaws snapping.

Prill screamed and ran up the stairs, but Tony just laughed and jiggled the head about on its pole. "Smashin' i'n'it?" he said to Molly, as she tried to close the door. "Best we've ever 'ad, I reckon."

"Prill won't eat hers," Colin said, looking at the plate of cakes on the kitchen table. "She's gone to bed, I think. So has Rose."

Molly couldn't think what to say, so she picked up her bun and took a small mouthful, to avoid talking.

Oliver also chewed away in silence, but he kept taking the currants out of his mouth to inspect them. They were awfully hard, just like bits of gravel. It didn't make sense at all. He'd helped Winnie to mix them and he'd seen all the ingredients.

Colin found a piece of bandage in his, but he spat it into the fire without saying anything. He thought the Edges had made the Soul Cakes, and nothing surprised him about that lot.

"Look at this," said Molly, with forced cheerfulness, picking something off her tongue. "What on earth—ugh, it's a *fly*. Honestly, I've eaten some funny things in my time, but this beats everything."

The church bell started a slow, monotonous tolling. Molly threw her bun on the fire and glanced up at the clock. "There's a service tonight," she said. "They're getting ready for tomorrow. All the Edges'll be there, you know they're killing really. They go round terrorising everybody with that horse, then they pray like mad."

"What's tomorrow, Molly?" Colin said, his mind going blank.

"Good Friday, dear."

"And it's St Elfin's Eve tonight," Oliver added firmly, but only to himself.

# Chapter Seventeen

Oliver made his preparations carefully, with the thoroughness of a man preparing for an African safari. He went to bed a few minutes after Molly had locked up, saying he was very tired and yawning his head off. But up in his bedroom he immediately came to life and checked through his small rucksack yet again—book, torch, spare batteries. Notebook, pencil, chocolate, thermos flask—empty, as yet. He'd have to creep down and fill it when everyone had gone to bed.

He was a creature of habit and usually slept with an alarm on the bedside table. But that might wake Colin. He got into bed fully clothed, snuggled down and closed his eyes; he would have to rely on his inside clock, it hadn't failed him yet. Whenever he wanted to get up early for something he always found himself wide awake, long before he needed to be. Let's hope it works tonight, he said to himself, closing his eyes and getting comfortable. Tonight of all nights.

It was chiming midnight when Oliver crept down the garden path. He was late. He needn't have stopped in the kitchen to fill a flask with cocoa, but he was going to need plenty of warm drinks if he had to stay out till two o'clock.

There was a big moon, with shreds of cloud sailing across its face. The crooked steeple looked alive as the shadows patterned it, like a crooked finger beckoning him on. He pushed the lych gate open and walked up the path. The graveyard was very peaceful and the mossy tombs were dimmed to soft round shapes against the knotted trees, like little old women talking together.

"Death is natural, Oliver," his mother had always told him; as a nurse she'd had to get used to it. "Bodies are just

144

like shells, dear. Little boxes that contain the human spirit. Think of it that way." He only listened to half his mother said these days; as she got older she tended to repeat herself. But he clung to it now because fear was plucking at him. There were so many graves, so much rottenness under the ground. He couldn't not think about dying, with Molly's friend Kath Brierley laid out at the undertaker's, all ready for her funeral.

She'd been young once, he'd seen a photo of her on the cottage mantelpiece. Why did people have to get old and worn out, anyway? Why did they die?

He sat down on a huge flat tomb on the left of the church door. It was only half-past twelve, and if he was really going to stay there for a whole hour and a half he'd have to get himself organized and keep himself awake. He ate two squares of chocolate and had a swig of cocoa from the flask, then he looked around. The churchyard slept under the quiet stars, little dark shapes scurried across the sodden grass, and he heard the odd squeak as some tiny creature met its end in the claws of a night hunter. Determined to sit it out he opened his book and switched his torch on.

But nobody, not even Oliver, could have concentrated on a funny story in those circumstances. It was ridiculous to have tried. He started his favourite "William" adventure, where the Outlaws put notices all over horrid Aunt Emily's bedroom, but he didn't get any further than William sticking the label on her big false teeth.

*"Harmes be to all who over churchyard pass,*
*Grim Death himself shall take the first and last."*

The strange lines were written large on every page, and even when he shut his eyes they rang in his head like great bells. He was crazy to have come here, just because of an old story. Had anyone ever done it before? He'd nearly asked Molly but he thought she might get suspicious and stop him.

The church clock suddenly struck one. Oliver jumped, dropped both book and torch, and shot bolt upright. It was pitch black now, the moon had been blotted out by swags of thick cloud, and he couldn't see a hand in front of his face.

*Don't panic Oliver. Find the torch and switch it on again, you twit.* But the bulb must have broken when it hit the path, and he clicked it on and off in vain.

He sat down again abruptly. There was a slight breeze now; perhaps, when it drove the clouds off, he'd be able to see again. Until then he'd better sit tight on this damp gravestone.

Had the Edges ever done this for a laugh? Had they ever sat in the graveyard on St Elfin's Eve just to see if there was anything behind that old saying? "No smoke without fire, Oliver." His father was always quoting that. He wanted someone there with him, even someone like Sid or Tony Edge. Panic had started to gnaw at his insides like a little worm. It was ridiculous, he must pack up and go back to Molly's. But Elphins was at the bottom of that hideous lane, with its dripping trees and its rustlings and its fantastic shadows.

He got colder and colder. Damp was steadily seeping through all his layers, his two pairs of gloves, his bobble hat, his thick scarf. In the end he forced himself to his feet and groped round blindly, trying to pack his rucksack. He'd make a dash for it down that lane in a minute. Anything was better than staying here.

Then something moved by the lych gate, a kind of fog, quite dense and white enough to make his eyes tingle, but with shapes behind it. *Or was it making itself into shapes?* Oliver stood rooted to the path in terror. His cold, aching body didn't belong to him any more, his legs refused to obey messages from his brain. He wanted to run but his feet had become enormous weights and his skin was clammy and pimply with nerves. His arms swung uselessly at his side like dismembered limbs.

The small, bright fog was moving slowly towards him along the path, silent, unhurried, bobbing about haphazardly like a big balloon, and as it came nearer Oliver could see that the blurred grey shapes inside were separating themselves into people.

A huge horse led the procession and the figure on its back was small and female; she sat side-saddle, with a full skirt billowing down, hiding all but the toes of her tight boots. Oliver looked into her eyes. There was something familiar about that young, unlined face. It was Miss Brierley, but as she had been seventy years ago, the same sweet face he'd seen in the family photograph. Old William looked no different from usual. "He was the loveliest old horse I'd ever seen," Prill had sobbed when she told them about the Head. He plodded patiently along the mossy path, whisking his ribboned tail.

Another figure shambled behind on a pair of crutches —Porky Bover with an enormous bandage round one foot, gamely making his slow way down the path and grinning at his own awkwardness, trying to hop. They were like figures in a dream, silent, intent upon their own small world, a passing show that neither heard nor saw him. As he stared, the enveloping cloud reached the church door, thinned out and dissolved, till all that remained of it was a sore, prickly feeling behind his eyes.

So it was true, and what it had told him was true. In a strange way the ghostly procession had given him comfort because it foreshadowed nothing that hadn't happened already. Kath Brierley was dead, so was the old carthorse, and Porky Bover had certainly suffered "harmes". Harms, but not death, thanks to the accident unit at Ranswick Hospital, and to the Edges.

Oliver stood up shakily. He would never tell anyone about this never ever. Let it remain a dream with Colin's midnight row on the lake. No one would believe a word of it anyway, even if he trusted them enough to share such a secret.

147

He took a deep breath and pulled up his anorak hood over his damp hair. The long, long night wasn't quite over yet, there was the lane to face. He would just have to make a dash for it, but at least the moon was out again.

And it was shining on something by the gate, a little grey shape that slowly became a person as Oliver began to walk down the path with his rucksack over his shoulder. It was a girl.

In his great relief he'd forgotten the second part of the old rhyme, forgotten that whoever came last was also marked for Death. Porky Bover was still alive and kicking, how could he have been so stupid to think that was the end of it?

The girl was in a hurry. She rushed anxiously along the path and swept past him in silence, urgently, as if she feared that the door might be shut in her face, and death denied her. He had a glimpse of thick, long hair as she passed into the porch, and he heard himself cry out desperately, "Stop! Please stop! Don't go in there!" Knowing it was useless.

He sank down on his cold tomb again, staring at the church door, willing her not to enter, then he looked up. The small ghostly figure was still standing there, and she was looking him straight in the eyes. It was Prill.

# Chapter Eighteen

"For heaven's sake . . . what on earth . . . *Oliver!*" Prill sat up in bed and put her hand over her eyes. "Switch that thing off, can't you. It hurts." She was staring at him in complete bewilderment, fuddled with sleep and very angry. He had switched the light on and was standing at the end of the bed, gawping at her like some prize idiot.

"I've . . . I've . . ." he stammered. "Are you all right?"

"Well of *course* I'm all right. But just what are you doing in here? It's—it's half-past two in the morning. I was fast asleep."

"I know. I'm sorry. Only something woke me up, and I thought—"

"Clear off, Oliver. It was the best night's sleep I'd had for weeks, till you came barging in. Go and take one of Molly's pills if you're so wide awake. There's no need to disturb everyone else in the house."

But Oliver didn't move. "I just felt like talking to someone," he said lamely, inspecting her with his large pale eyes. She *looked* normal, a bit hot perhaps, but not as though she was sickening for something.

"You felt like *talking* to someone!" she repeated incredulously. "So you come and disturb me, in the middle of the night. You're cracked!"

"Prill, I—"

"CLEAR OUT!" And she picked up the nearest thing to hand and flung it at him.

Oliver fled, only just managing to pull the door shut before a shoe crashed against it. He felt peeved; Prill had changed since they'd come to Stang, all her gentleness had gone. He'd quite liked her before, she'd always been more patient with him than Colin was, and less disapproving, but she had no time or patience for anyone now. It had all started after she'd seen the horse's head.

He scuttled back to his own room and got into bed, then he lay awake for a long time, worrying. Any normal person would have asked him what he wanted; you didn't usually go round waking people up in the middle of the night. If she'd asked, he'd have tried to explain and they might have got somewhere. But Prill had gone away from them now, she was totally absorbed in her own little plans to get out of Stang. Wherever she went from now on, he decided, he would have to go with her. It wasn't going to be easy though.

The Friday morning dragged terribly; Oliver trailed round after Prill and irritated her to death. "Stop looking at me, you creep!" she yelled at him, brushing him away like some big bluebottle. He had insisted on helping her and Rose chop up vegetables for a stew, and he watched eagle-eyed in case the knife should slip and his cousin sustain some terrible injury. She was like the princess who was doomed to die by pricking her finger on a needle.

Oliver never did anything by halves. Unknown to Prill he spent an anxious hour on guard duty outside the bathroom while she took a bath and washed her hair. Molly didn't have one of those non-slip rubber mats, or handles to help you get out of the bath, and he knew quite well that you could drown in a few inches of water. But she sounded happy enough, humming pop songs and listening to the radio. Her mood was lightening because she was going riding in the afternoon, and Jackie Bostock's company always cheered her up. He couldn't stop her going, she'd been talking about it all morning.

Colin was going too. They decided not to remind Molly about her promise to drive them to the stables. She'd been landed with all the arrangements for Kath Brierley's funeral and Elphins had suddenly filled up with undertakers and vicars, and decrepit relatives of "the

150

deceased". So they swallowed lunch in record time and ran down to the Green to get the one-thirty bus. Just as the driver was moving off someone pelted across the road and scrambled aboard, panting noisily. It was Oliver.

"Thought I'd come too," he said in an embarrassed voice, heartily wishing he'd not said anything about his fear of horses.

Their very size frightened him, he hated their great bloodshot eyes and he loathed their smell. He'd been the one toddler on the beach who always refused a donkey ride along the sands, and here he was, planning to shell out all his cash for an expensive riding lesson.

Prill stared out of the window and ignored him. She was thinking about her mother and father, and about Alison. Oliver could do what he liked so long as he didn't tag along after her all day. But Colin was puzzled. Uncle Stanley was very mean with Oliver, and he never had much money to spend; besides, he'd told Molly he was nervous of horses—she'd tried to persuade him to go riding herself. "Will your mother mind, Oll?" he said casually, as Oliver counted the money in his little brown purse. "Only, well weren't you planning to go to church or something?"

Oliver went red. She certainly would mind, and he'd forgotten. It was Good Friday, and she'd have taken him to a long, dreary service at St Matthew's, if he'd been in London. She wouldn't have let him watch television, or ride his bike or anything, and she'd be bound to ask him about Stang Church when he got home. She could be very disapproving at times.

"I can go tonight," he said firmly, knowing perfectly well that there would be no evening service. "I don't see what difference it makes. There's nothing else round here to spend my money on anyway, and . . . and I've always wanted to go riding," he lied.

Colin didn't say any more. Oliver was working up to something, he was like a saucepan coming up to a slow boil. He'd driven Prill mad this morning, creeping round after her like a lunatic, asking her if she was "all right" every other minute. He must have come to spy on them, or perhaps he wanted some more information about Porky Bover's accident. He was very interested in grisly stories. Perhaps he was planning to sneak off to the hospital to get the gory details from Porky himself. Whatever he was up to, he must think it was very important. Oliver was like his father, he didn't part with his precious money easily.

Getting him mounted was quite hilarious, and even Prill smiled. When he saw the string of ponies, saddled and bridled and ready for the off, Oliver backed away. Even the small ones looked enormous, and a couple of them were eyeing him suspiciously and tugging at their halters.

Jackie Bostock gave him a leg up on to a little furry black thing called Paddington, but she could see he was nervous. "This one's always half asleep, Oliver," she whispered in his ear. "He won't give you any trouble. Now, are you comfortable? Take the reins . . . no, like that . . . good. That looks fine." Paddington took one step forward and Oliver let out a little yelp. Behind him Colin and Prill collapsed into giggles. "Look, I'll take you on the leading rein for a bit," Jackie said loudly, winking at the other two and mouthing, "Shut up." "Now we've got to find a hat that fits properly. Miss Trent's very strict about that."

Oliver really made a meal of it. The first hat came right down over his ears, the second was much too small, and he said the third and fourth had a funny smell. In the end, Jackie got quite annoyed. The Blakemans had arrived late and their two hours were already eaten into. She wanted a good ride this afternoon, and there was only so much time to waste on this nit Oliver. Prill was right, he *was* pathetic. She didn't understand why he'd wanted to come anyway.

He calmed down a little when they were on the move. The horses walked at a slow pace out of the stableyard and along the lane, and Paddington didn't buck or rear and throw him off in a fit of bad temper. He was a fat little pony and kept stopping to eat grass from the verges. Jackie showed Oliver how to jerk the reins and keep them short. "Let him know who's boss," she advised him, and he started to get the hang of it after a while, though the whole thing struck him as extremely boring.

Prill was two horses ahead on a brown mare. "She rides well," Jackie told him, not realising what sweet music this was in the ears of the anxious Oliver. "She's got a natural seat and no nerves. The horse can always tell." It was a good thing his own greedy little mount was so dozy then, Oliver decided. Every time a car came past his stomach turned over, in case Paddington got frightened and bolted.

As they ambled down the green lanes a watery sun came out. The trees and hedges were loud with birdsong and it felt quite warm. Up at the front Colin unzipped his anorak. "I'm hot," he shouted back. "First time I've been really warm since we arrived."

"It's going to be a lovely Easter," Jackie said to Oliver. "I wish we hadn't got to go away, I'd much rather stay at home, this time of the year. You're lucky to be staying with Molly, Stang's a gorgeous village."

He didn't answer that. It wasn't a bit like this in their dark little hollow. The sun never seemed to warm it up and you never heard the birds singing. There must *be* birds, but he hadn't been aware of the usual chirruping and arguing that came with spring, even in towns.

Jackie decided to take them to the wishing well on Saltersly Moss. Miss Trent, who owned the stables, had packed them off on their own, with Jackie in charge. She was busy getting ready for an Easter gymkhana and she was only too pleased to have the horses exercised. "Are we allowed?" Oliver said anxiously. "She only said, 'down the lanes'." He always stuck to The Rules and he wondered how far off this place was, and whether they'd get back in the two hours. He couldn't afford to pay for extra time. Besides, the longer they were out the more risk there was to Prill. He wanted her back at Elphins where he could keep his eye on her.

"It *is* down the lanes," Jackie told him. "There's nothing much to see, but it's quite pretty. Well, it used to be, I've not been for ages."

"Wishing well" sounded quite romantic and they all had their own ideas about it. If he could have one wish, Colin decided, he'd use it for Porky Bover. He couldn't stop thinking about him, with his foot trapped under that mower. Rose had been quite right in what she'd told them, he'd checked with Molly. They'd had to give him a second blood transfusion before he was "out of the wood". *Please let him get better*, Colin said to himself. Please let everything be all right.

Prill was thinking about her parents, against hope that nothing would stop them coming down from Scotland on Easter Tuesday. They'd phoned to say they were now leaving the Camerons earlier than they'd originally planned. Mum hadn't said why, but Prill thought Molly had got something to do with the sudden decision. She was banking on Tuesday anyway. *Don't let anything stop them*, she pleaded silently.

Oliver couldn't take wishing wells very seriously. In any case he had to concentrate on Prill. But he did feel more relaxed. It was such a lovely day and they must be out of the danger zone, up here. By now the Edges would be tearing round the village, getting everything ready for tonight's big dress rehearsal, and enjoying another barney about Porky Bover's replacement.

Then, from somewhere across the fields, a church bell started tolling. Oliver started guiltily, and thought about his mother, down on her knees in gloomy St Matthew's, in one of her awful hats. Paddington trotted for a few steps and he wobbled dangerously, then they slowed down again.

Yes, it was right to be out here in the fresh air, jogging along the lanes with his mind fixed firmly on Prill. It *felt* right. *Please don't let anything awful happen*, he begged. Wishing was a bit like praying really, not that his mother would understand that.

Saltersley Well was the big build up for the big letdown. The approach was pretty enough, down a great sweep of hill with huge trees on both sides of the road, meeting over their heads in a dark green tunnel. But the well itself was filthy, and choked with litter; the sandstone sides were cut to pieces with initials and things like "United for the Cup" and "Val loves Eddy" and "Kevin Bates Rules O.K.". And the whole place smelt horrible.

"Sorry, folks," Jackie said, wrinkling her nose. "It's obviously gone down the nick. It was awfully pretty once though, we used to come here on picnics."

"Well, it must have been a long time ago," Oliver said tactlessly.

Jackie took no notice. She was getting rather irritated by this fussy young boy who squeaked like a petrified rabbit the minute his pony showed the least spark of life. She suddenly unfastened Paddington's rope halter and put it in her pocket. "You can walk back on your own, Oliver," she told him. "I'll ride Meg, and we'll stay behind you. O.K.?" Meg was the big grey she'd been leading with her other hand. Before he could protest, she had leaped up on to the broad back and was wheeling the horse round. "Let's give them all a drink," she called to the others. "Then we'll go back. There's plenty of water anyway."

The horses drank greedily from a ditch that had overflowed its banks and was seeping all over the road. Nearly every head was down, and the riders were chatting to each other, when something appeared over the brow of the hill and began coming towards them at great speed.

Only two of them saw it—Oliver, who was yanking Paddington away from a clump of lush grass, and Prill, whose chestnut had drunk its fill and was now snapping irritably at the heels of the horse in front. At first it was only a little dot, silver and blue, flashing in and out of the leafy shadows, then it became a person hunched over low-slung handlebars, squealing with fright as the bicycle ran away down the long hill, helplessly ringing the bell and applying the brakes, then sticking his feet out.

With nightmare accuracy the machine cannoned straight into the knot of horses, hitting two mid-on. Colin found himself cantering down the lane, Meg shied away, neighing loudly; Paddington, feeling a sudden slackness in the reins, cashed in, dropped his head and began tucking into the verge. But Prill's horse, caught in the belly, reared up in terror. Its head went back and its front hooves splayed out wildly, thrashing the air. Prill lost the reins, the stirrups dropped away and bounced against the great flanks, and, as the horse reared for the second time, she was flung off backwards and fell straight down, hitting her head on the road.

The demon bike rider was Sid Edge. As the dust cleared he got to his feet shakily, retrieved his cap, then looked up dumbly at the forest of legs, piebald, black and white, jostling and wheeling about as the riders reined in their frightened horses and Jackie tried to calm everyone down, before another took fright and bolted. "It's these brakes," the boy was mumbling, sounding rather bewildered. "I reckon they need tightening. Jus' didn't work. There must be some screws missin'. Me dad'll have to have a look. Brand new an'all." Then he saw Prill, hatless, out cold in the middle of the road. "Hey, is she all right? That's your sister, i'n'it?"

She looked dead. Her head was lolling over at a horrible, twisted angle, and all the colour had been sucked out of her face. From one corner of her open mouth a thin dark thread fell slowly down.

No one took any notice of Sid Edge. Colin didn't even hear him. Numbly he obeyed Jackie Bostock's icy instructions as she dismounted and covered Prill with her riding jacket. "Get off, and lead your horse over there, by

156

that gate. Keep your eye on Oliver. There's a farm up the road, I'll phone from there. *Don't touch her, whatever you do*," and she'd gone.

Oliver, who was usually so cool in a crisis, was shaking so much that he could hardly stay on the pony's back. His reins were on the ground, getting all tangled up in its hooves. He didn't notice Sid creep sheepishly over, shove his bike in the hedge, and sort them out for him. His eyes were fixed on Prill's yellowy cheeks, desperate for the tiniest movement. In the awful quietness the little red worm reached her chin and dropped a tiny bead on the road.

He shuddered and closed his eyes. It was his fault, he should have locked Prill up. He'd heard about horrific accidents like this, they could happen to the most marvellous riders. If only he'd told them about last night, if only he'd not pretended to Prill that he'd been walking round because he couldn't sleep. She just might have listened to him.

Now it was too late. It had been a terrible fall; she'd crashed down on to the road like a stone hurled from a great height, with all the strength a man could muster. People could die from quite small blows to the head. If Prill died it would be his fault.

# Chapter Nineteen

Life gradually took on the tangled quality of nightmare. The two boys couldn't remember just how they got to places, or who spoke to them, and the hours and days got hopelessly mixed up. At first Jackie Bostock was with them, then she went away and her father came, and they seemed to be sitting endlessly in cars and offices and waiting rooms while time crawled by, like something half dead.

Now they were sitting on a hard bench in a room with sickly green walls, while a phone call was put through to Molly Bover. But there was no reply, and Colin couldn't remember Judge Cameron's number. A stream of doctors and nurses passed in and out of big swing doors, and there was a lot of mumbled discussion behind raised hands. Phone calls were whispered so they couldn't make the words out, and a uniformed figure flitted over to them from time to time, uttered some polite, meaningless remark, then went off again.

They were not allowed to see Prill, and in the end a doctor suggested they went home. Everything possible was being done, he told them, and the hospital was trying to contact Mr and Mrs Blakeman. "We can only wait," he said cautiously, in reply to Colin's hoarse questions. "There's a taxi outside, ready to take you to your aunt's. Mr Bostock's arranged it. Off you go now."

The kindness of the elderly driver was almost unbearable, and he embarked upon a gentle prattle as soon as they were through the hospital gates. "Little girl's had a bump on the head, has she? Well, that's nothing to worry about. My two lads play rugby and they've been in and out of that hospital half a dozen times, I should think.

Marvellous those doctors are. Now don't you worry. She'll come round, and then you'll wonder what all the fuss was about . . ."

In the back, Colin reached out and silently took hold of his cousin's hand. Oliver was still trembling and he felt extremely cold. He'd hardly said a word in the hospital, except something ridiculous when Jimmy Bostock arrived, something like "my fault".

He stared out of the window as the budding hedges swished past, seeing nothing but that small face in the road, the cloud of auburn hair, the slow trickle of blood. His hand lay in Colin's like a dead fish, his china-blue eyes were red and sore, and his pale cheeks were smudged with tears. Colin opened his mouth but the simplest sentence was beyond him now. He turned away and looked out of his own window, pressing the tears back, and the dreadful chatter of the taxi man went on and on.

When they walked through the front door of Elphins, Molly was speaking to the hospital on the phone. The tiny hall was very narrow and she more or less filled it. As they pushed past she put a hand out and touched them both.

The tears ran down Colin's face. He muttered an excuse about fetching something from his bedroom, and ran upstairs two steps at a time. Oliver looked as if he was cracking up, and Molly had to go to her best friend's funeral in the morning. Someone must keep cheerful. He gave his face a good wash and blew his nose thoroughly, then he went back downstairs feeling oddly light-headed, as if he'd got flu.

He confided how he felt to Rose. "Shock, that is," she said calmly, shovelling three spoonfuls of sugar into a mug of tea. "Here y'are, get this down you. Sweet drinks are good for shock." The dogs, catching the general mood, were trailing at her heels, hoping for scraps. When nothing appeared, Jessie hobbled over to Colin and slumped down on to his feet. His father would see her soon, thank heaven she was making a good recovery.

Though however bad her limp was, he doubted that either of his parents would notice now.

Molly spoke in clipped, short sentences, as if she was keeping herself on a very tight rein. The hospital had only told her what the two boys already knew. Prill hadn't broken any bones but there was a massive blow to the head and she was deeply concussed. "They can't tell us any more than that, dears," she said, busying herself over the tea things. "We must just keep cheerful, that's all. For Prill's sake."

But her mirthless smile fooled nobody. Oliver wanted to know if they'd managed to contact his aunt and uncle. He was dreading that. He was fond of his Auntie Jeannie and he remembered vividly how she'd gone to pieces last summer, when the baby fell ill and they couldn't get a doctor. He didn't want the police to find them yet.

It appeared that they'd gone touring for the weekend, in a hired car, because the judge and his wife had decided to go to Edinburgh, to stay with friends over Easter. An S.O.S. message was to be put out on the radio that night before the ten o'clock news.

"In a way it might be better if they didn't get here till she comes round," Molly said thoughtfully, echoing what was in Oliver's mind.

"But *will* she come round?" whispered Colin, spelling it out at last.

"Well of *course* she will, lovie. Look, you've got to believe that, Colin." And Molly put her arm round him, and tried to make him eat something.

His tears flowed freely then, and Oliver pulled up a stool on the other side and sat staring dully at the tablecloth. At their feet the dogs huddled together, the poodles whimpering in sympathy. But Jessie was growling uneasily—she didn't much like the funny noise that Colin was making. Rose brewed fresh tea and banged the pot down on its stand, making all the crockery rattle, and down in the village the church clock began a miserable tolling. "It's Good Friday," she said savagely.

They all went upstairs very early, closing their bedroom doors and resigning themselves to a long night of lying awake. No one had wanted to stay downstairs any longer, the old house was too heavy with their unspoken thoughts, and whenever the phone rang there was a sickening wait as Molly ran into the hall to answer it. But it was never the hospital.

At one in the morning Oliver went down to the kitchen to refill his hot-water bottle. The low-ceilinged room, with its cooking smells and its copper pans, was very comforting. He made himself some Ovaltine and sat drinking it at the table, with his small bare toes buried in the silky hair on Jessie's back; that was comforting too.

Molly had tried to cheer Colin up by showing him his photos of the play rehearsal. "Kwik Flicks" had done them in twenty-four hours, in time for the Easter holiday. "He deserves to get on, that young man does," she'd murmured approvingly. "Let's have a look then, Colin."

But he'd been disappointed. The photos were no better than Oliver's efforts, worse if anything. They were all dark and rather blurred, and none of the interesting details showed up properly. He just couldn't understand it because he'd been extremely careful, and his flash had been working.

"What a pity," Molly had said sympathetically. "Do you think you need a different kind of film, dear? Only this kind of shot is always—"

"Oh, it doesn't *matter*, Molly," he'd snapped at her, shoving all the photos back in their envelope. "They'd have been hopeless anyway, people kept moving about."

"But they've cost you so much money, Colin . . ."

161

"I said it doesn't *matter*," he'd repeated desperately, the hopeless tears for Prill creeping into his eyes again. What did a few old photos matter, compared with her? What did anything matter?

Oliver sipped his Ovaltine and spread the twelve photos out on the table, then he looked at them for a very long time. Had Colin seen what he could see now? *No*, he decided. There'd been no terror in his voice, no wild alarm, just a great weariness that told everyone to go away and leave him alone.

His brain was running ahead so fast now he felt quite feverish. So much was spinning round inside his head, so many dark threads were coming together into one awful whole, that he no longer knew what he saw in the pictures, or what his mind made him see.

And he realised quite suddenly that there was no difference now, and that it didn't matter any more. He adjusted his thick glasses and brought the photographs right under his nose, examining them minutely, one by one.

Every single shot was marked by the outline of a face, but it wasn't contained in the features of the Mummers—in Tony arguing with Winnie Webster, or in Uncle Harold preening himself in gold and black. The pictures themselves were faces. Out of the blurry darkness, broken only by the top of a blond head or a flash of white arm, the hard, harsh lines that had become so familiar to him leered out yet again. This was the face in that hedge where he'd seen the dunnet, this was the face on Rose's embroidered horse and the face on the doll that Colin had hurled into the pit. This was Sid's face as he stared down at the unconscious Prill, opening and shutting his mouth like a fish.

Oliver stared and stared at the twelve photographs, and his heart turned to ice inside him. Molly's old pine table had become a treeless heath, and across it hobbled a filthy old beggarman, limping away from an ancient city whose people had hardened their hearts against him. He heard the gates clang shut, he heard the terrible curse and the waters rising, and he saw how the old man's face changed slowly from meek hopefulness to murderous, blistering hate.

Then he looked back at the drowned city, and he realised that the face of the keeper of the gates and the face of the beggar were one and the same. His curse had not withered and died in the waters of Blake's Pit, it had grown and flourished like some monstrous tree, bearing no fruit, but tainting unborn generations with its evil, with its power to trick, and maim, and kill.

He burned the pictures in the grate, then dragged himself up the creaking stairs with a feeling of utter helplessness. Tomorrow, perhaps, he should burn all his other "proofs". What use were they to anyone now? Who could put out a hand and stop what was happening?

A great darkness had reared up out of the waters of that pit and had brought death in its train. Not just the death of a tired old woman but the cruel death of a young girl who had the whole of life before her. Officially Prill was still alive but she may as well die now, tonight. There was no hope of life for her at all, not any more.

Mr Blakeman rang at breakfast time and spoke to Molly first. "No change, no *worse*," she whispered over her shoulder, scribbling on a pad and explaining apologetically about Kath Brierley's funeral. After a minute she gave the phone to Colin. "We're in Carlisle," Dad said, "and we should be in Ranswick by about eleven. Meet us at the hospital." The pips went but he didn't put any more money in, he wanted to get back on the road. Colin ached. His father had sounded so bright, so normal, it was Mum who sometimes panicked. He was looking forward to seeing his little sister again anyway. She was such a comic and she had such wicked ways. Alison would cheer anyone up.

The chatty taxi driver was coming to drive them to the hospital. Molly went to Stang church early, to wait for Miss Brierley's relatives, and the two boys stood in the road, looking out for the car. Preparations for tomorrow's Mumming were already underway, and the horse's head was propped up in the Edge's window with all the chops and sausages, gay with green and yellow ribbons, its thick new varnish gleaming. Colin looked away. There was a last rehearsal planned for tonight and the grand performance was to take place tomorrow, after Evensong. He was glad they couldn't go now; Prill had hated the play from the very beginning. She'd told Winnie Webster she thought there was something terribly wrong with it, though she didn't know what.

When they got to the hospital they discovered that Alison wasn't there. "Your mother just felt she couldn't cope with her," Mr Blakeman explained in an embarrassed voice, "and she wanted to be quite free, for Prill. So we've left her in Scotland for a couple of days. She adores Mrs Cameron, she calls her Nanna."

Colin was taken aback at first, then puzzled, then rather resentful. Sticky-faced Alison was normality, and he associated her with Prill. They needed life around them now, not all these stage whispers and this unnatural politeness. What was the point of Mum being "free for Prill" anyway? She was totally unaware of anybody's existence.

He just couldn't get through to his mother. When they arrived she was sitting alone in Prill's room and all he could see of her was a patch of brown hair and a few inches of blue coat framed in a little glass panel. His sister was surrounded by pieces of bleeping equipment, monitors and charts—a small pink blur against a mountain of white. Colin didn't want to look at her in the middle of all those tubes and wires, it made him want to scream.

When Mrs Blakeman came out she gave Oliver a quick

hug, but she kept her arms round Colin for a long time, staring past him into space. It was like being embraced by something half dead. He'd only seen his mother like this once before, last year, when Alison had been very ill.

They all went to the hospital canteen and had cups of coffee, but Oliver and his uncle did most of the talking. Mr Blakeman asked a string of questions about the holiday, about Stang and Molly Bover, even about the riding stables, and Mrs Blakeman seemed to be listening quite intently to Oliver's carefully considered answers, but with dead eyes. Oliver's behaviour was eerie, too, he was much calmer than yesterday and there'd been no more tears. He'd withdrawn into himself, just like his aunt. You could tell them both that black was white now, and they'd listen.

Just as Oliver was telling them about the Mummers, Mrs Blakeman drained her coffee cup and stood up. "That's very interesting, Oliver," she said politely, "but I must go back to Prill now, I'm afraid," and she simply walked away in the middle of his sentence.

Dad tried to gloss it over and went for some more coffee, but Oliver was bossily flapping him into silence. It was his uncle he really needed to talk to. "Prill's very sick, isn't she, Uncle David?" he said, the minute his aunt had disappeared. He wanted to add, "She's going to die, isn't she?" but he didn't, not with Colin sitting there.

For a moment Mr Blakeman didn't answer. This child always disturbed him somehow. He was so adult, so knowing, you could never tell him half a story about anything. Their own children were so much more straightforward.

"Head injuries are always tricky, Oliver," he said at last. "I'm sure you know that. She's not broken any bones or anything, and her skull's not fractured. It's just concussion, terribly severe, obviously, and doctors can't

165

make predictions in a case like this. They daren't. She's holding her own, and that's all they can say."

"It was my fault," Oliver burst out suddenly, in a strangled voice. "I made a fuss about the riding hats, and Prill ended up with the wrong one. That's why it came off when she fell."

"Oliver, don't, *please*. That's ridiculous. I'm sure the hat had nothing to do with it. They don't protect you in every case, you know. The whole thing was a freak, the steep hill, that boy's bike going out of control. He's in quite a state apparently. The mother keeps phoning up."

But Oliver's glassy look told him that the boy wasn't listening. "Look," he said finally, "I think perhaps you two ought to go home for a bit. There's nothing you can do here, and sitting around just makes it worse for everyone. Come on," and he gave his son a pointed stare. Oliver was beginning to get on his nerves now, with these wild theories about the accident, and he needed all his reserves to cope with his wife.

"Molly'll be glad to have you at home for a bit," he said, shutting the door of the taxi. "She can't have had a very jolly morning."

"You'll phone, won't you, Dad?" Colin mouthed through the glass, as they drove away. It was the same taxi, the same old man, the same tortured Oliver sitting beside him. Yesterday had become today, and nothing was better.

"I promise. Off you go now," Mr Blakeman said.

But there was only one phone call before bedtime, to tell them that there was still no change. Colin wouldn't ring off until he'd got his father to promise that he'd come and collect them in the morning. "I don't want to stay here, Dad," he said in a whisper. "Can't we stay with you at the hotel?" Then he went up to bed, taking Jessie with him, and fell asleep with his arms round her neck, dreaming about giant horses and riderless bikes,

166

and shiny coffins being lowered into the ground in Stang churchyard.

Oliver didn't want to go to sleep, and he didn't want to go back to Ranswick either, not now. There was too much to think about and plan, and he wanted to stay in the village. The riding accident had pulled all the blurred edges into focus at last. Everything that ghostly procession had foreshadowed was true, except for Prill's end, and that too was happening, even as he lay there.

Through his open window came snatches of song and laughter. The Mummers, wild and noisy after their final rehearsal, were being turned out of the pub. And tomorrow night they would perform their play. Tony would take the King's part, an Edge would play it instead of a Wright, and the ancient pattern would be broken for ever, all because of Winnie Webster's well-meaning arrangements. Did she really know what she had done? Did anyone?

The Wrights had always been respected in this village. Most of them had been farmers but some had become schoolteachers, and one had gone into the church. His father knew the family history. He knew all about the Edges, too, with their history of lies and cheating, and about the two brothers centuries ago, two highwaymen who'd been hanged on a gibbet on Brereton Moss.

Tomorrow Sid and Tony Edge would fight against each other, evil against evil, and it would be more than play-acting. The one would strengthen the other's arm as they wrestled and hacked and slashed, and the hands that were already round Prill's throat would tighten for ever, dragging her down . . .

As Oliver drifted off to sleep his fingers loosened at last on the text of the play, and the crumpled pages dropped from his hand as consciousness left him. He knew now what he must do, and why they had come to Stang. He at least must stay there. Through the cold night, and on into the colder dawn, the boy slept peacefully.

# Chapter Twenty

Easter Sunday dawned, cheerless, cold. All over England village bells rang out with the message that Christ was risen from the dead, daffodils blazed in gardens, and here and there in Stang churchyard, half-opened buds gleamed pallidly. In her small room off Ward 5A, in Ranswick Hospital, Prill Blakeman lay motionless; her parents sat by her bed, side by side like two stone figures, blank-eyed as the grey light touched the windows. There was no change.

Molly didn't phone the hospital and she was less cheerful now. She ordered the boys to wrap up warm and get into the car while she took the dogs round the village. She was going to drive them into town herself, there was no need for Mr Blakeman to come. Rose Salt was left with a list of instructions about dogs and dinners, and they saw her looking rather pathetically through the front window as Molly reversed down the drive, peeping at Tony Edge who was letting himself into the Stores, with bulky coloured bundles under his arm, for the play no doubt.

Molly seemed to have difficulty steering a straight course. On the main road several cars hooted at her and a van driver unwound his window and swore. All her calmness had gone and she seemed rigid with tension; her pleasant, low voice was now a tight whisper. Oliver hadn't dared suggest he might stay at home for the morning, not with Rose slamming down plates of egg and bacon, and Molly snapping at her, and Colin all white and silent turning his food over, then pushing it aside uneaten.

He would have to change his plan of campaign slightly, so he took his purse with him. He also took the precaution of unpinning the bus timetable from the back of the kitchen door and slipping it into his pocket. There was unlikely to be a bus on Easter Sunday, but if there was he didn't want to miss it. If need be, he'd have to come back in a taxi.

At the hospital Molly spent a few minutes in Prill's room talking to Mr Blakeman; then she went home. She didn't speak to the boys again, and her round, moon face was a mask, thickly-lined and old. "She seems so angry with us," Colin whispered to his cousin, as the untidy figure vanished through the swing doors. "She's almost behaving as if it's *her* fault . . ."

"Don't worry about it," advised Oliver, in a cool, contained little voice. "People often behave oddly when something like this happens. They feel guilty, you see, when there's trouble." He nearly said, "when people die", but he bit it back.

Mrs Blakeman was asleep in the hotel room. She'd been sitting by Prill's bed most of the night and she'd nodded off in her chair. Oliver decided to find out where Porky Bover was. They might let him into the ward for a few minutes and he could try and get to know a little more about the accident. Besides, there was no point at all in staring at Prill hour after hour. The Blakemans would cope better if they stayed away for a bit, in his opinion, but he didn't dare say so.

Mr Blakeman thought how sensitive Oliver was being, stealing away somewhere so he could be on his own with Colin for a few minutes. He'd not told Molly but there'd been an alarm during the night, a hideous few minutes when bells rang in Prill's room and doctors and nurses came running, and they'd been asked to go and wait outside.

But she'd "stabilized" again, whatever that meant. "I know they mean well," he told Colin wearily, "but I wish they wouldn't treat us as if we were subnormal. I'd rather know exactly what's happening, however bad it is." They were sitting together by Prill's bed. Surrounded by all

169

those tubes and wires she looked like something from a monster pop-up book. Colin glazed his eyes so he didn't have to look at her. "How bad is it, Dad?" he said at last.

Mr Blakeman couldn't speak, but a tear rolled slowly down one cheek. "I don't know. They don't really tell you anything. They *can't*. You know what it's like, they watch her all the time, they keep checking those machines. I . . . I feel like pulling all the plugs out and smashing them up sometimes."

He looked at Prill, tiny in the high bed, and suddenly saw Judge Cameron. When you spent long hours concentrating on one face everything about it became etched in your memory. He'd not enjoyed doing the portrait much, the look in those small, hard eyes was proud and self-assured, and there was a harshness in the mouth. Why hadn't he painted Prill instead?

He stared helplessly at the pale white oval against the big pillows, at the thick red hair straggling down. A nurse had come in and brushed the ends of it this morning, and she'd chattered to Prill about Easter eggs, as if she could hear her. There she lay, hour after hour, like a sleeping statue, innocent, lovely, slipping away from them.

Colin squeezed his father's hand. "I'm hungry, Dad," he said. "Let's go back to the hotel, it's ages since I ate anything." He really wanted to get his father away from the hospital for a while. He'd been quite cheerful yesterday, but now he was becoming distant and preoccupied, like Mum, only hearing half of what people said, and only half responding.

He went to fetch Oliver from Porky's ward on the floor below, but the patients were eating their lunch and the nurse told them he'd gone twenty minutes ago. "Perhaps he's at the hotel," Mr Blakeman said, but Colin was suspicious, and when they got to his mother's room he wasn't really surprised to find a note from Oliver propped against the bedside light. "Didn't feel very well," the spindly handwriting informed them. Went back to Molly's for a bit. Will come in later if possible. Sorry. Oliver."

Mrs Blakeman was coming round after the doctor's sedative, complaining that she felt a bit sick but wanting to get straight back to Prill even so. Mr Blakeman was hovering round her anxiously. Colin crumpled the note in his hand. He was disgusted with Oliver and he knew why he'd sneaked back to Stang. It was the play.

He simply didn't understand this weird cousin of theirs. Since Prill's accident Oliver had been through every mood in the book, quite hopeless when it had first happened and a bag of nerves for hours afterwards, unable to stop blubbering on about it. Then he seemed to have pulled himself together again, he'd become calm and thoughtful, trying to jolly the others along with his rather trite remarks. Even Molly had asked him to be quiet.

Now he'd deserted them. He'd done his level best to secure a part in that play, but when he'd failed he'd started laying plans to get there early. He was going to sit right at the front, he said, and take some "action shots" for his father. Prill's accident had put going to the play out of the question, of course, and to Colin's amazement Oliver had actually said so, last night, and rather wistfully too. He simply didn't behave like normal people.

Oliver Wright was no better than the Edge family. Grown-ups were often quite impressed with him, but deep down, Colin thought he was callous and calculating. He told lies sometimes, to get what he wanted. This note was a lie and it meant he'd deserted the Blakemans, with Prill in that ghastly hospital, lingering between life and death. Colin never wanted to see or speak to him again.

Oliver was lucky; there was just one bus going to Stang that day and he'd caught it in the old market place. It got stuck though in a big traffic jam, just beyond the roundabout, and after that everything crawled along at a snail's pace. When the police eventually waved them on, Oliver could see a car crash involving three vehicles, and a van lay in a ditch, hopelessly flattened like an old tin can. How could anyone come out of that alive? He wished he'd not seen it, not with Prill so desperately sick in Ranswick Hospital. It was more than he could bear.

The bus didn't hurry, and its leisurely progress down the country lanes gave him more than enough time to think of all the strange things that had happened in Stang since they'd come to Molly's. He didn't want to think of them at all, but they wormed their way into his head like a life's memories when someone goes under the water for the last time, asking all the useless questions that nobody would ever answer. Why had Sid Edge's bike hurtled down the hill at that precise moment in time, and why couldn't Prill have fallen another way, on to soft grass? Why had that silly poodle crept into the kiln and what had prompted Sid to shut it in? Would the police ever find out what had happened to Posie Massey? Who closed the door on Colin, and how had his dog been hurt when there'd been nobody on the tower? His mind revolved endlessly and grew tired, and he could make no sense of it.

Oliver was nervous of dogs, but Jessie was rather a beautiful one and she limped now. It was not meant to be, no more than people were meant to hobble about with sticks, or to have withered limbs, or to become mortally sick and die.

"Ta ta, George," the driver shouted, as an old man got off the bus by a lonely gate. Through the open door Oliver caught the scent of a wild flowering tree, and he could hear the birds singing. Just for a minute his heart lifted. These were the lovely things. But in that dark village the poisoned waters of the pit were tainting man's very existence. The old curse lived on, and through one family, so that everything people did was fated to go horribly wrong. Nothing flourished in that valley any more, not even spring.

He knew he must keep out of Molly's way for the afternoon, in case she pounced and asked him awkward questions, but his luck was in. Aunt Elsie Dutton always came to the play, and Molly was going to keep her promise and had gone over to Brereton Cross to fetch her. "She'll stay to her tea," Rose said. "They won't be back till half-past six. That's what she told me, any road."

It was perfect. Oliver now had all the time he needed to go through his lines and to find out exactly what the Mummers did on "the day". There'd be ritual attached to that too. Rose knew the drill precisely. At about four o'clock they would all go to Pit Farm for a big high tea. On a fine day they'd jazz around the village in their costumes and knock on people's doors with their collecting boxes, scaring the children with Old Hob. But just after two it began to pour down. "They'll not come out in this," she said sadly, peering through the window. "They won't want to get wet. We'll have to wait now."

She disappeared into her bedroom and didn't emerge for an hour and a half. Oliver stayed in the kitchen with the dogs, going through the play and trying to keep warm. Then a little cough in the doorway made him turn round. Rose was standing there shyly. Or *was* it Rose?

This young woman was rather beautifully dressed, she had a long skirt of red wool and a dark pink blouse. "Molly gave me these," she whispered, fingering the patterned sleeve. "She knows I like nice things."

"You . . . you look fabulous, Rose," Oliver stammered. Everyone laughed at Rose Salt, but just at that moment he felt more like crying. The Edges would be too busy trying to remember their lines to take much notice of her tonight. But don't let them laugh at her, he pleaded silently. He had realized what was different. She was no longer wearing the knitted brown pixie-hood.

Dark brown hair, soft and quite curly, had fallen down on to her thin shoulders. "Do you think she's bald, Oliver?" Colin had said, that first night, and they'd sniggered away up in the bedroom.

"There'll be a queue to get in," she said solemnly, looking at the clock. People come from all over to Stang Play. I'm going across at about half six. Are you coming?"

Oliver hesitated. "No . . . well, not quite so early anyway. You go, Rose, when you're ready. Get a good seat."

He was glad of the rain. It fell steadily into the valley hour after hour, as if someone up on the Heath was pouring it out of a bottomless bucket. The wind got up and howled, the sky was thickly overcast, and Stang suddenly went into hibernation. Children were called home, cottage doors were shut, and it became a dead village as people lay under hatches and waited for the play. "Won't make no difference," Rose assured him, smoothing her skirt. "Folks'll still turn up, you see."

The most crucial element in Oliver's plan was the monstrous red bike. All afternoon he was on tenterhooks, willing Tony not to move it from the rusty shack behind the Stores where he usually tinkered with it on his free afternoons. And luck was on his side. When he stole down Molly's path, just after five, it was still there.

He'd had dreams about what he might do to that great grinning machine; he'd like to attack it as if it was all the Edges that had ever been. He'd like to stick red-hot pokers into its wheels, and dent all its shiny chrome fittings, and cut a great hole in its petrol tank to see all the petrol gush out. But he knew he couldn't. The police might get involved if he did anything like that, then there'd be real trouble.

All that was really necessary was to flatten the tyres, and Oliver systematically unscrewed every valve he could find and waited for a sudden rush of air. When nothing seemed to be happening he took out a pair of scissors from his trouser pocket and plunged them twice into the rim of each wheel. The blades were small but extremely sharp, and he'd pinched them from Rose's sewing-box that afternoon. Now, at last, the tyres were really going down, and with quite a satisfactory hiss. But Oliver hadn't quite finished. He was puny, with muscles like knots on cotton. Nevertheless, he managed to lug the machine away from the wall, and with one great shove he pushed it over and left it in a heap amid a litter of oil and rags.

Feeling quite giddy with his success so far, he left the bike where it was and went on into the shop, squeezing through a tiny window at the back and jumping down into the smelly storeroom where they made sausages and mince, and where Colin had been trapped inside the chiller. He felt quite bold all of a sudden. He could probably have tampered with the lock and got into the front shop, but this wasn't going to be necessary if his luck held. The night was young and there was no point in wasting energy.

He found the old wooden wedge, undid the meat safe door and propped it open a couple of feet. Then he wrought havoc, pulling down bundles of paper bags from a shelf and spreading them all round the floor, upsetting two cartons of baked beans, heaping old cardboard boxes in the middle of the room, then jumping on them. When he was satisfied that it looked like a proper break-in he unlocked the door and went outside again. It was nearly six o'clock. In a few minutes the Mummers would be coming down from Pit Farm to get dressed in the school room. The last part of his plan was definitely the most tricky.

Tony Edge was extremely stupid. He got the shock of his life when Oliver, in his sopping green anorak and with water dripping off his hood, stepped out from a gateway and said, "Psst!", then put a cold hand over his mouth. "What the *hell* . . ." he began explosively, but the hand

175

didn't go away, not until the posh little voice had told him someone had been tampering with his bike, and that it thought whoever was responsible was doing more damage in the shop.

It was still pouring down and the Mummers were fast disappearing in the murk. "Hey!" Tony yelled. "Hey, *Dad* . . ." But the wind was howling. It snatched away his words and flung them back down the valley towards Blake's Pit. Oliver felt half drunk, with nerves mainly, but also because he saw the gleam of success. He felt reckless. "I'd come on your own, Tony," he whispered in the large ear. "A large crowd might scare him off. Besides, it'd be good if you could spot him in the act. On your own, I mean . . ."

And Tony Edge smelt glory. He crept up the hill after the little green gnome, went round the back of the Stores and followed the boy's shaking finger from his motorbike up to the light in the dirty window, which Oliver had thoughtfully left on. When he saw his bike lying in a heap, with both tyres flattened, the youth let out a roar and began to swear. "Shut up!" Oliver whispered frantically. "You don't want him to get away, do you? Here, give me that." Tony needed both hands to pull the bike up off the floor. He handed Oliver the rolled-up costume and tugged till his precious machine was upright again. Then he wanted to examine it minutely, and squatted down on the dusty floor, determined to find out just where this maniac had slashed the tyres. He'd slash *him*, in a minute . . .

"Come *on*, Tony," urged Oliver, still holding on to the costume, and tucking it right under his arm just in case Tony asked for it back. "There isn't time for that. I don't know what he's been up to in there, but the place is a shambles. he's after the big joints of meat, I should THINK—all the turkeys and things . . ."

The youth fell for it and stared round-eyed at the mess on the storeroom floor. His uncles would kill whoever

176

had done this. People had nicked joints from the shop before, but they'd never wrecked the place. Silently, Oliver jabbed a finger at the open door of the meat safe.

"In there?" Tony mouthed, creeping towards it.

"Well, the light's on," Oliver whispered back. "Let's—"

"Oh, get out of the way," the youth said rudely, shoving the boy aside. Whoever it was must be still in there, helping himself. He didn't want this little twerp to interfere now. This was a man's job.

It gave Oliver immense satisfaction to kick the wedge aside and shut Tony in the chiller. The play wasn't very long, so he wouldn't die, and it might cool his temper a little. He paid no attention at all to the muffled yells and hammerings, but shook out the baggy white robe and looked at it thoughtfully. It was very long and he'd need all those pins he'd borrowed from Rose Salt's sewing-box. As for Tony Edge, he wasn't going to waste any more time on him. It was only tit for tat, after all.

# Chapter Twenty One

A long queue of people were now shuffling into the old schoolroom. The tiny playground was flanked by a low wall, and Oliver was behind it, crouching down in the muddy darkness, listening carefully to all that was going on. The play always began at half-past seven. "And not a minute after," Frank Edge told Winnie, through the door of his cardboard grandfather clock. One of his parts was Old Father Time and the costume was made of two big cardboard cartons painted brown. "Our Tony's missing," Jack Edge muttered through his hood, taking a swipe at Jason as he careered up and down the rows of iron desks, hitting people with a pig's bladder tied to a stick. "Damned if I know where he is."

"Oh, he'll have forgotten something," Uncle Harold grunted, looking rather menacing in his black and gold doctor's tunic. "I saw him going back down the hill. He's not on at the beginning, any road. I'll send our Vi to see what he's playing at. He'll be back. Stop meithering."

At seven-thirty precisely, one of the Puddings crawled out from under a bench and struck up a tinny gong. Winnie stepped forward and cleared her throat nervously. She was dressed in a curious floppy garment with huge sleeves that looked rather like a dressing gown. There was some feeble clapping, and a weak cheer from the back.

"Ladies and gentlemen," she began, "Just before we start I thought you would like to know that our young friend Porky Bover is making an absolutely *splendid* recovery. He wanted to be here tonight but, er, well, naturally, he has to stay where he is for a few days. His part will be taken by his father Eric, a *stalwart* member of our team, you'll remember, till Porky took over three years ago. One or two other changes have been made but we now have a full cast again, and I can assure you that they have all worked *very hard*. So, without further ado, let the play begin. Over to you, Mr Bover . . ."

As Porky's father came forward with his broom, Winnie stepped across the thick chalk line that circled the acting space and plumped down near Molly with a sigh of relief. "Thank goodness that's over," she whispered, and settled down to watch. Now that it had started she would take no further part, unless someone needed prompting. Everything would happen inside that thick white circle, and whatever mishaps occurred, nobody would dare to interfere. It was the most ancient rule of the play.

Molly wasn't listening. She was squashed up on a hard school bench next to Rose and fat old Elsie Dutton, wondering what Oliver was up to. She'd been going to give the play a miss and spend the evening at the hospital with the poor Blakemans, but the father had phoned just as she was putting her coat on, to ask if the child was *feeling better*.

She'd been deliberately vague and reassuring, but she didn't have a clue about Oliver's whereabouts. Then it occurred to her that his disappearance might have something to do with the Mumming. He'd been fascinated by the whole thing since the day they'd arrived. She couldn't see him in the audience though. Fortunately, the performance never lasted very long, and when she found him Molly intended to give him a big piece of her mind.

The play got off to a noisy start, with Porky's dad pushing at the people in the front row with his witch's broom, yelling, "Room, Room, Gallons of Room," and with Frank Edge capering round inside his cartons and bellowing:

*"Here come I,*
*Old Father Time,*
*Welcome or Welcome not,*
*And I do hope Old Father Time*
*Will never be forgot."*

And he banged two pan lids together, to imitate the sound of a clock.

Uncle Harold stalked about pompously, showing everyone what was inside his huge black bag. There was a saw covered with thick red paint, some giant pincers for pulling teeth out, a heavy wooden hammer and a big glass bottle. He showed everything to the audience with great ceremony, but the most important item was the magic medicine. Whenever somebody got killed the Doctor was called for, to pour a few drops down his throat. At this point he always said exactly the same thing:

*"Here, take a little out of my bottle*
*And let it run down thy throttle.*
*And if thou be not quite slain,*
*Rise Sir Knight and fight again."*

When these lines were delivered, whoever was lying "dead" on the floor, stiff as a board with his toes turned up neatly, pantomime fashion, got up and ran off into the "dressing room", miraculously cured.

The play went through its motions with all the usual hiccups. Sid Edge, a small but sturdy figure in his purple Slasher costume, demolished three coloured knights in quick succession with his knobbly rubber club. Old Father Time wept each time a man died, the Doctor ran on with his magic potion and repeated his little chant:

*"A drop on his head and a drop on his heart*
*And up he rises to do his part."*

And the "dead" man walked off, amid stamping and applause from the audience.

At one point the action stopped altogether and the Mummers all looked at Winnie. A slow hand clap started at the back. "Lights . . . lights . . ." somebody whispered, and the schoolroom was plunged into darkness. Then a chant began, "Old Hob, Old Hob, Give him a tanner, Give him a bob," and a single spotlight revealed Frank Edge, running round in his tatty cartons, shoving the shiny, grinning skull of old William into the faces of the squealing children. This was the part they liked best.

In the excitement, Jason Edge crashed into a desk and got a nosebleed. Things ground to a halt for a second time as he sat wailing in the middle of the chalk circle, saying he didn't want to be Little Devil Doubt any more, and where was his mam? The lights promptly went off again while his father sorted him out, and Old Hob leered and dipped at the audience, his ribbons and streamers brushing across their faces like invisible cobwebs.

After some confusion Jason was restored to his mother, and Slasher stood alone in the middle of the "stage". He had now killed St Patrick, St David, and St Andrew, Robin Hood, Oliver Cromwell, and a man all in yellow called Great Walloping Jack. Once more he issued his famous challenge:

> "Slasher's my name, The Prince of Darkness I,
> With my club and my sword
> I all men do defy."

A shiver went through the audience, and those that were familiar with the play waited for the big moment. Now the dressing room door would open and admit King George, who would storm on and make mincemeat of him.

But the familiar white-robed figure didn't come out of the little kitchen, where the players waited when they weren't on stage. It was making its way up the hall from the main exit, carefully picking its way between the rows of iron desks, and stepping into the charmed white ring. The Edges were bewildered. Our Vi had run all the way back from Pit Farm and reported that she couldn't find Tony anywhere, and Harold had been all set to alert Winnie and ask her to stop the play for a minute. Now he'd suddenly materialized from nowhere. Well, *somebody* had.

They knew that it wasn't Tony the minute he opened his mouth, and anyway, this man was far too short. The white robe, with a red cross slashed on the breast, hung on him in great folds, and he'd already tripped over his pinned-up hem. But nobody laughed and nobody stopped him. Nobody could. It was as though the rough chalk circle had sent up great steel walls to keep out intruders. The Edges peered at each other through the slits in their masks, and at the two small figures facing each other across the dusty floor. They were bewildered, and for the first time rather frightened, and a strange silence had fallen upon the whole room, as if a sorcerer had cast a spell.

King George delivered his lines flawlessly, in a thin, reedy voice which was trying hard to imitate Tony Edge's flat Cheshire bleat. "But it's *Oliver*," whispered Winnie, and made a move to get up. She would have to do something about this, circle or no circle. Where in the world was Tony Edge?

"Leave him," Molly said, in a strange voice. She understood now. She saw more clearly than Winnie Webster with all her years of study and her knowledge of Mumming, and she watched carefully as Oliver levelled his big wooden sword at Slasher's middle, held up his red and white shield, and uttered his great challenge:

"*George is my name, King George that slew the
    dragon of old,
This shield bear I stronger than iron or gold.
With this do I defy all manner of evil,
With this I lay in dust world, flesh and devil . . .*"

At the word "devil", Oliver lunged at Sid. He didn't intend to let him spoil things now, by running away or by revealing that he wasn't Tony.

*"Tremble thou tyrant, for thy sin that's past*
*Tremble to think tonight shall be thy last . . ."*

As he yelled, he dropped the shield, took his sword in both hands, and gave Slasher a great wham with it across the knees.

"*Ouch!*" Sid cried, hopping up and down. He was too frightened to do anything but stand there and try to fight back. Whoever it was must be some kind of loony; he knew it wasn't Tony. Perhaps it was someone from the Saltersly troupe, gate-crashing on Stang Play. They'd tried that once before. There was no need to overdo it though. "Give over, will you," he hissed, as Oliver chased him round the circle. "You really hurt me that time, mate. Trying to kill me or something?"

But King George appeared to have gone mad. "*I'll spill thy blood, thou black Moroccan dog!*" he howled, and when Sid backed off he kicked sword and shield into a corner, then grabbed the rubber club and flung it into the audience, amid great cheers.

But this time Slasher was ready for him. Inside that dark hood Sid had had a change of heart. If he wanted a fight he could have one. The Edges weren't going to be shown up by some sneak from Saltersly Mummers. He pushed his flowing sleeves up, away from his wrists, and bared his knuckles. Oliver did the same. With a gasp from the mesmerized spectators the two figures met and locked together in a tangle of purple, white and gold.

Inside the baggy costume, Slasher's wiry little body was tough and unyielding, and he returned Oliver's punches with iron fists. His first blow hit King George on the mouth, and the soft hood that covered his face did little to soften the impact. Oliver went tottering backwards, feeling the warm blood spurt between his teeth, and hit his back on one of the old desks. The audience gave a suppressed roar. The King was out of the circle, but he bounced into it again, like a boxer coming off the ropes, and went for Sid with both hands, feeling for his throat underneath the purple folds, and digging his nails in hard.

Sid jerked his head back and tried to break free, tearing at Oliver's face, determined to rip the hood off and expose this maniac, whoever it was. But suddenly, a foot went out and neatly hooked his left leg from under him. The small purple figure crashed down on to the splintery boards, so heavily, and with such a cry of pain, that the audience let out a little cry of sympathy. This was some fight.

Within seconds both the knights were on their feet again, and each was trying to push the other over. Sid hurled himself bodily at Oliver in an effort to topple him, but although he was much lighter, and not half as strong, the miniscule King George stood his ground, like a sturdy little tree buffeted by the wind. He met every blow the other boy dealt him, he anticipated every trick. Time and again the grunting, sweating Sid attacked him with fists, nails and palms; time and again Oliver met him stoically and turned the blow away, with skills he didn't recognize as his own, with courage he didn't know was in him.

The fight couldn't have lasted longer than five minutes, but it felt like Oliver's whole life. In the end it was dream-like and calm, as if he'd left his body far, far behind, and sat looking down on the magic ring from a great height, while down below two tiny robed figures sweated and heaved and strained in silent anguish. They didn't spill each other's blood, they felt no pain, all they were conscious of was the power between them, coming together like two enormous tides, then falling back only to meet and shatter again like the waves of the sea.

Oliver's mind was full of dragons and deeps. The waters threshed and boiled in it like the waters of Blake's Pit. But when the flood had ebbed away he could see that it had become a cool, echoing cave, whose mouth had been sealed up with rocks and mossy stones. Above his head the world turned slowly, and a huge, bright figure, all the colours of Superman, had his hands locked round it, trying to slow it down on its axis. At last it stopped, and at the same moment all the boulders rolled away, bouncing down the mountainside, and a figure walked out of the cave into the bright sunlight, a small figure with a rope of auburn hair, in a hospital nightgown.

He came out of his dream to find he was trying to sit on Sid Edge. He'd managed to push him right over, but the stocky little figure was still endeavouring to get up. His hood had come off, and the round bullet head was jerking up and down, as if wired to his shoulders with a spring. In the end, Oliver actually lay on top of him, and stared up at the ceiling, totally exhausted. Someone threw his sword back into the ring, and he managed to catch it. As Stang clock started to strike, King George pulled his own hood off, flung it away triumphantly, and held his sword up to the roof.

What a fabulous ending! It was the best fight the audience had ever seen and they started to clap and cheer enthusiastically. But then Slasher's head fell back for the last time and hit the floorboards with a sickening crash.

Just before eight the Blakemans had been summoned to Ranswick Hospital. They had been in the hotel since six o'clock, trying to eat a meal and sitting like zombies in front of the television screen. Their ears were sore with listening for the telephone bell, and they were hoping against hope that it wouldn't ring. Then it did. When he heard it Colin's heart lurched horribly, and he saw his father feeling round for the car keys as he spoke to the hospital.

"They want us to go," he said in a grey voice, putting down the receiver. "Just me and Mum."

"Can't I—"

"Stay here, Colin. It's no use. You'd be better not coming."

"Is this it, Dad?" Colin said in a dry whisper, grabbing his father's sleeve as he hustled Mrs Blakeman towards the lift. Everyone had used words like "going" and "sinking" about what might happen to Prill. Their grandmother talked about people "passing away" "Death" was like a rude word.

"Is she going to die, Dad?" he asked in a loud unnatural voice. There, he'd said it at last. The very sound of it gave him cold shivers. And his father turned back in the hotel corridor and said, "Yes," just like that.

But as they sat yet again by the silent hospital bed, something was happening to Prill behind the lifeless mask. It was as if she was coming back along a little black road, all on her own after some great journey. At first it was very quiet, then a bird started cheeping up in a tree, and she heard a soft beating noise which gradually became louder and more distinct, and which she finally recognized as a church clock.

The country she passed through was desolate. Nothing was very clear, because her eyes were tired, but there were signs of great struggle under the earth; heaps of broken rocks, and rivers that had burst their banks, and trees all twisted and broken by rushing winds. But she knew for certain that the land had survived its great battle, that she too had survived, and now she was being drawn on, and upwards, to what looked like a single point of intense white light.

As she got nearer, the light expanded. It was no longer round and complete but had opened out like the petals of a flower and was bathing the whole earth. This light had the strength of steel and the power of the sea. It was so great it seemed to be pushing her on to her knees with the force of a great hand. Prill knelt down, but that was not enough, so she stretched out on the hard, black road and lay with her face hidden from it, in case she went blind, but knowing that she was still alive, feeling frightened and mystified and glad.

Her eyelids flickered. The light in the ward was hard and bright and she felt sick. Suddenly a clock chimed somewhere in the town, and a man's voice was saying, "Everything's happened in medicine, Mr Blakeman. I admit that we were worried half and hour ago, but I . . . Well, what can I say? What can anyone say? Sorry to have alarmed you like that, but in a case like this it could have gone either way. Everything will be analysed of course, and we'll make a full report. No doubt you'll be interested. Thank God it's turned out like this, anyway."

"Mum?" the girl in the bed was saying. "*Mum*?" It didn't sound like her voice though. This girl's voice was all woolly and peculiar, as if she had pebbles in her mouth.

"What? Prill? Are you feeling better now, love?" It didn't sound like her mother either, and it didn't look like her at all. This face was all red and ugly, from crying.

"I'm so *hungry*, Mum," the girl in the bed said, in a clearer voice this time, and she sounded rather cross about it.


On Easter Tuesday, Prill Blakeman and Sid Edge were brought back to Stang in the same ambulance, which was embarrassing to say the least. Slasher hadn't responded at all to Uncle Harold's magic potion, or to Winnie's furious prompting from the front row. Old Dr Eliot had been in the audience. When Sid didn't move he'd pushed to the front to have a look at him, and pronounced that he'd knocked himself out. He came round eventually, but they packed him off to Ranswick Hospital "for observation". Oliver had done his job better than he knew.

Prill hadn't wanted to be separated from her parents, or from Alison, not for a minute. The Camerons had brought the little girl down from Scotland the day before, and now Prill kept getting glimpses of her through the back window, in the little red hired car, waving and yelling and burying her sticky hands in her mother's hair. "You'll be more comfortable in the ambulance, dear," the ward sister had advised Prill, "you'll be able to stretch your legs out. The other children can travel with you if they like, and you'll have Sid to talk to."

Colin and his cousin sat side by side, opposite the two invalids, but never exchanged a word. Oliver was in disgrace. In the relief of Prill's recovery Dad had said very little about his sudden disappearance, and Mum seemed extremely vague about it—she had quite enough to think about anyway. But Rose Salt had gossiped. Winnie was very cross with him for playing that extraordinary trick on Tony Edge, and she'd argued with Molly, who seemed to think it was all rather hilarious, a kid's prank of some originality. The Edges weren't speaking to anyone, of course, and were threatening to go to the police.

Oliver didn't care. He sat with his hands thrust in his pockets and thought about the play. How glorious it had been, in those last few minutes. Sitting on top of Sid Edge had made everything worthwhile. From the string and bus tickets in his left pocket he pulled out something crackly. It was his photo of the hedge with the rare bird in it. He glanced down at it slyly. It was a rotten photograph, all blurred with a little brown splodge in the middle that might have been anything. How could he have taken it for a dunnet?

He would burn it when he got back, and he'd burn his copy of the play too. That was all over now. The one thing he wanted to keep was Rose's little gold horse which his fingers had closed on in the other pocket. It was so pretty, joyfully prancing across his palm, he'd like to keep it really. Still, it belonged to Rose and he ought to give it back. There was nothing in its face to frighten her now, or in Sid's either. He just looked tired and a bit bewildered.

It felt much warmer down in the valley, and when the man stopped outside Elphins and opened the ambulance doors, a sweet smell came in, a smell of flowers and grass and blossoming trees. It was beginning to feel like spring at last.

"Gorgeous house, Molly," Dad said, getting out of the car and looking up at the moth-eaten thatch. "Gorgeous village altogether, actually. I'd like a look round later, when we've got Prill organized. Now cheer *up*, Colin," he called across to his son. The boy was so irritable and gloomy, you'd have thought his sister was still at death's door.

Nobody could understand why he was being so foul to his poor cousin; he'd completely ignored him in the last twenty-four hours—it was quite embarrassing. Oliver couldn't be expected to feel quite the same about Prill as her own family did, and he'd been amazingly helpful and considerate to everyone since she'd come out of hospital, a real paragon of good behaviour.

They went home two days later. Molly felt lonely afterwards, it was so quiet. She'd enjoyed having the old house full of children. When the car had disappeared from sight she stood by the gate, still waving sadly into the dusty silence. They had all waved and smiled, even Prill, but Oliver had waved longest, flapping his small white handkerchief through the back window.

And it was Oliver she remembered. He wasn't like the other two, she'd known that from the beginning. Life in the village had been plodding and ordinary before he'd come to Elphins, but things had started to go wrong on his very first day. The two Blakemans hadn't had very much to do with what had happened, she was sure of that. Oliver was the one, there was something *about* him.

The Edges were responsible for a great deal of course, they were weak vessels, easily led and easily tempted, always ripe for new evils to work upon. But something must have activated them this time, something must have entered the quiet valley and unconsciously triggered off that appalling train of events. All was peace, before Oliver came.

She stared across the road and saw Sid Edge fiddling with his bike outside the Stores, and her mind went back to the night of the Mumming. She saw Slasher draped in purple and gold, and the little white King with a cross on his breast. All the villagers said it was the best play they had ever seen. Only·Oliver had understood that the fight in the shabby schoolroom was a fight to the death.

But none of this would ever mean very much to the bewildered Colin. They were squashed in the back of the car together, all the way home, but he never said a word to him, and it was a very long time before Oliver was in his good books again. Colin found it hard to like him after what he'd done, and he never really understood why he'd deserted them when everything was at its worst, and why he'd sneaked off, just to be in that awful play. And Oliver never explained.

# Afterword

Although you will not be able to find Stang on any map, its Mumming play is real enough, and part of a very old tradition. These plays are still performed occasionally, in English towns and villages, but you would be quite lucky to find one nowadays, for they are part of a rural way of life that has almost passed away.

In the 1950s, I used to go "Soul Caking" in a Cheshire village. To me this simply meant watching, with other children, as a Mumming play was acted out in a country schoolroom. It wasn't until years afterwards that I understood that "Soul Caking" referred to the little cakes of corn which were eaten at harvest time, a ritual act symbolizing the taking in of life and strength from the "corn spirit", and from the souls of the dead. "Our" play, I remember, was always performed round Hallowe'en, All Souls Night.

I don't remember eating corn cakes, but I do remember the play, with its all-male cast, and the air of secrecy and excitement which hovered over all the preparations. I remember the warring knights, and Beelzebub, and the comical Quack Doctor with his bag of outsize instruments and his magic potion, which always brought the dead men back to life again. Above all, I remember the hobby horse, and that awful, thrilling moment which we waited for every year, when the lights were switched off, the schoolroom was plunged in darkness, and the jaws were snapped at us again and again, while we all squealed with delight.

"Old Hob" is a special feature of Cheshire Mumming and takes the plays far back in time, beyond the dawn of Christianity, to the rituals of ancient horse worship. An authentic hobby horse would be made from a real skull. Here is a description of the whole process, from somebody who clearly knew all about it!

"The horse's head never belonged to Lymm. It belonged to Warburton and was always kept at the Saracen's Head, and Garnett Bauff hired the costumes for the young men of Warburton. The first horse's head was stolen, so two of the men went to Toole's of Warrington and got another head and they boiled it in a boiler at the "Saracen's Head" and got all the flesh off it. They had to put it together again and glued the teeth in, painted it and decorated it and put it on a wooden leg and put a handle at the back to open its mouth and the man underneath the cloth worked it."*

The plays were traditionally performed at set seasons of the year, Hallowe'en, Christmas, and Easter. But although Christian elements have crept in over the centuries, they remain essentially pagan. There are dozens of variations, both in character and staging, but one great theme underlies them all. It is the symbol of death and rebirth, the ending of the old year and the beginning of the new, the harvesting of the ripe crop, and the hope of fresh life and growth to come.

A.C.

*Extract of a letter from E. M. Leather to Mrs Yarwood, 8th November 1950, published in The English Mummers and Their Plays (Alan Brody, Routledge and Kegan Paul, 1971).